When Ash Remains

By

DENA GARSON

DEDICATION

As always, to my boys.
.

1

The buffalo bull stopped eating the grass at his feet and lifted his head. His flank quivered as he scanned the surrounding area.

Kajika remained motionless and silent in the tall pasture near the river bank.

He felt certain his fellow hunting party members would recognize the buffalo's unease. They certainly didn't want to spook the herd. A stampede could get one of them hurt. Or worse, killed.

They were close to replacing their tribe's food stocks from the winter and spring months. He didn't want to risk any of their hunters now. Especially when they were about to enjoy the rewards their work had brought them. If they were able to take down even three from this herd, they would all have extra meat and skins to trade with neighboring tribes.

Kajika waited until the large bull he was stalking returned to his meal, then crept forward. Not a sound could be heard as he closed in on his quarry. Every warrior in their tribe envied his stealth. The elders alleged he could sneak up on death himself. It had taken many seasons to hone that ability, and he took considerable pride in it.

When he came to the edge of the grass that had kept him hidden, he found a comfortable position to ready his attack. He double checked that the knife strapped to his thigh was unbound and ready to be pulled from its sheath, then notched an arrow in his bow.

He sighted the vulnerable spot just below the bull's throat and waited. As soon as the giant bull lifted his head to swallow the grass he'd been chewing, Kajika let the arrow fly.

As he raced after the arrow with his knife in hand, a war cry passed through his lips.

His fellow warriors leapt from their hiding places and pursued the buffalo that scattered across the river. The chaos that ensued likely appeared to be pure madness but in actuality followed a well-practiced routine.

As Kajika wrestled with the bull, he sensed Tuari, one of the younger warriors, moving in behind him, protecting his back. Now he didn't have to worry about one of the bull's herd helping their leader instead of fleeing.

Sweat slicked Kajika's chest and back as he danced out of reach of the creature's horns. When he saw an opening, he leapt to the side and landed a blow of his knife to the creature's softer underbelly.

The bull roared out in pain and whipped its massive head around, nearly spearing Kajika with a horn. Their morbid dance lasted for what felt like an eternity before the creature collapsed at Kajika's feet. He sucked in two lungfuls of air to steady himself before putting the animal out of its misery with one last cut of the knife.

Stepping back, he took in the scene around him.

The other warriors had brought down three of the females and were gathering supplies to move the carcasses.

Their efforts had been momentous. Each of the men in their hunting party carried his own weight, and they all worked together without infighting. The result was a successful hunt and ample food for their village.

Chief Yonaguska would be pleased.

Tuari handed Kajika a bladder of water and nodded to the downed bull. "He had a lot of fight in him."

"Yes, he did." The cool water relieved his parched throat.

"You always managed to stay one step ahead of it. Almost as if you knew what it was going to do next." The young man paused. "Did you?"

Kajika regarded him. Several flippant answers came to mind, even as he saw the almost reverent way the boy-turned-man looked at him. At the last minute, he said simply, "No." He took another drink. "No, I had no way of knowing what the creature would do next. I did what any other warrior would do." He looked the young man in the eye. "I watched the bull's ripple of muscle and where his vision went, and I followed my gut."

"It's as simple as that?"

Kajika checked the blade of his knife to make sure it hadn't been bent or chipped during his fight. "It's never a simple thing. In the heat of the moment when you're fighting for your life, you don't have time for a misstep. If you guess left and the creature you are hunting goes right, you could end up with a horn through the heart."

Tuari winced. "I did think he was going to catch you with his horn."

Kajika smiled. "I thought he might too."

"So are you telling me it just takes practice? That I have to get cut up a few times to learn how to read my prey?"

Kajika cocked his head and considered what he'd said. "Yes, unfortunately that is what it takes."

The young man took a deep breath and released it with a sigh. "That's what grandfather keeps telling me."

Kajika marched to the tall grass to retrieve the bow and arrows he dropped before engaging the bull. As expected, the young man followed closely behind. "The hardest thing you will ever learn is how to listen to your gut and trust what it is telling you."

"Truly?"

"Absolutely. Some men never learn to do that."

"Can you teach me?"

Kajika stopped prodding the grass for his things. "I'm afraid that's another thing you have to do on your own."

"Grandfather said I should just watch everything you do and then try to do it the same way."

Kajika shook his head. "That will only help you in certain instances. Others, you need experience to draw from and the confidence that your gut will never lead you astray."

"How do I know if it's my gut or just wishful thinking?"

Toe to toe, he took in the young man's ever-hopeful expression. "Again, practice." He gestured for him to follow. "Take some time before the winter hunt begins and walk through the forests alone. Watch the creatures and anticipate where they will go." With a glance in the boy's direction, he reminded him, "Follow them. See where they go and how they move. Tell yourself the rabbit will dart

3

to the left. Eventually you will feel an answer bubble up from your chest. Remember that feeling. Notice how often that answer is correct."

He dropped his weapons not far from the bull then rummaged through their things for the water skin. "Eventually those answers will be right more often than they are wrong. And when it is, you'll know you can trust them."

Tuari nodded.

"Now." He re-sheathed his knife in the holder strapped to his leg. "How about retrieving my pack while I rinse off in the river? When you return, you can help me ready this beast for our journey home."

Tuari's eyes shone as if he had been given a treat. "Shall we say the blessings to the Great Spirit for his generous gifts or have you already given thanks?"

Kajika barely refrained himself from sneering. There was no point wasting his time. He learned a long time ago the Great Spirit, or whatever you called it, didn't care about anything he had to say. "Go ahead if you want. I'm going to clean up."

If his attitude surprised Tuari, the young warrior hid it well. "Should I use the honeysuckle vine to tie up the skins when we're done?"

Kajika shook his head. "We will not skin it here. That can wait until we reach the village. Besides, Winema would be disappointed if she learns we found some of the vine she likes so well but then used it before she could even see it."

"Oh. I didn't realize it was for our chief's wife."

"Apparently the vine can be used to make hardy baskets." Tuari's cringe made Kajika grin. "There's nothing wrong with making baskets. Someday you may find yourself a wife who wants nothing more than to sit beside your fire and weave baskets. And you may become perfectly content to help her."

"I'd rather skin a dozen buffalo. Alone."

Kajika chuckled and clasped Tuari on the shoulder. "We shall see. Now, go gather some elm branches and my pack so we can begin our journey home before the setting sun."

When they arrived in their village, the sun had dipped below the tree line. The young were asleep in their beds. Yet Chief Yonaguska and his wife, Winema, greeted them near the main fire.

"Something is wrong," Kajika muttered.

"What do you suppose happened while we were gone?" Chea Sequah, one of his closest friends, asked.

"I don't know, but it can't be good."

"I had hoped we might have a celebration when we returned with our packs overflowing, but it looks as if that celebration won't be happening," Yansa, one of the other warriors, remarked.

Kajika steered his horse next to the fire and dismounted. A boy ran to his side to take the reins so he could properly greet the chief. He made his greetings then remarked, "I am surprised you both are so anxious to hear of our hunt."

Yonaguska clasped Kajika on the shoulder. "We are most anxious to hear. From the looks of it, your hunt was successful." With a wave, the Chief indicated he wanted Kajika to follow.

Kajika held back the questions he was anxious to ask.

"Death visited our village while you were away."

Kajika steadied himself for the worst. "Who?"

Yonaguska stopped and faced Kajika. His mouth had been set in a grim line. "Ghigau and her child."

Kajika's gut clenched. Ghigau was his cousin's wife. "How is Dyami taking it?"

"No one knows. He cannot be found."

Kajika's frown deepened. "He's not in the village?"

"No." Yonaguska scanned the area around them. Seemingly satisfied with the lack of additional ears, he said, "Ghigau was found this morning. One of the women expected her before the early meal, and when she didn't come, the woman went looking for her." He grimaced. "It looks as if a wild animal attacked them. However, nothing in their tepee was disturbed. None of their food or the skins drying just outside. Nothing that an animal might have been looking for."

As disturbing as the image was, Kajika asked, "What of Dyami?"

"The last anyone saw of him was when he left to hunt for rabbits for their evening meal. That was not long after the noon meal yesterday."

"He's been missing for more than a day?"

"It appears that way."

"And no one knows where he went?"

"No," Yonaguska admitted.

"What has been done to find him?" Kajika knew he was

pushing the limits of formality with his chief, but he needed to know everything he could if he was going to track his cousin.

"I sent men to search for him. They were unable to find him or any sign of where he went beyond the fields."

"None?"

Yonaguska shook his head.

Dyami was a skilled hunter, but he was a large man and heavy footed. He should have been easily tracked, even by an inexperienced pursuer. "That doesn't make sense," Kajika mumbled.

"None of this makes any sense," Yonaguska agreed.

"What can I do?"

"I want you to find out what happened and who or what is responsible. The women of the village are afraid. Some of the men too. They believe a wild beast is loose in the area. The children aren't allowed out to play, and no one wants to tend to the animals or the harvest."

"They need answers."

"Yes."

"I will find them," Kajika vowed.

"I know you will."

2

Ahyoka lay on the bank of the river, watching the branch of the overhead tree sway in the breeze. The leaves rustled and told her the story of Mother Birch. The insects, busy collecting bits of seed and drops of nectar, added their parts to the tale. The birds chirped from within the depths of the branches and provided a harmonious background chorus.

Her eyelids became heavy, and her mind drifted into the land of dreams.

She walked through a crowded forest. Trees were tangled and overgrown. The overhead canopy was thick and full and blocked most of the light. Her feet were bare. Every twig and rock she stepped on made her journey painful as she picked her way through the dense growth.

In the distance a wolf howled, making her hair stand on end. She stopped and listened so she could determine if the sound drew closer.

As she searched for the path she thought would be somewhere nearby, she heard the crunch of a twig from behind her. She turned but saw nothing but trees, leaves, and vines. Another snap of a branch from the same direction kicked her heartbeat up and sharpened her senses.

A growl hinted she was no longer alone. Without bothering to look over her shoulder, she took off running as fast as she could, scrambling over roots and twisted limbs.

Pounding footfalls warned she was being pursued.

The panting of an animal over the sound of blood pounding in her ears spurred her on. Seeing a clearing, she altered her course, keeping her eyes trained on the sunlit cove. As she neared the opening, a warrior stepped from the shadow of a large tree.

Even from a distance she could see his shoulders were broad and his chest was a solid wall of muscle. The feather he wore at the back of his head branded him a warrior of the highest honor.

He held a bow notched with a single arrow. As she drew closer, she realized the arrow was pointed at her.

The look on the warrior's face was of total calm and concentration. Something in his stance warned her that where he aimed, he wouldn't miss.

Just as he let the arrow loose, she woke with a start.

Awake Spirit Talker.

A man.

He watches.

A man.

He comes.

A man.

He hunts.

Ahyoka listened to the sounds of the spirits around her. Even without their warning, she would have sensed the presence in the shadows.

She rolled to her side and looked to where she knew he crouched. The darkness hid his features from her eyes, but his spirit radiated from the fire that burned within him. Never before had she met someone with such a potent life force.

Even her brother's wasn't as intense as this man's, and her family descended from a line of powerful shamans.

Did he mean her harm? Or was he just passing through?

Without taking her eyes off the place where he hid, she groped behind her for the knife she had been using before she dozed off. The apples she ate sat heavy in her belly as she contemplated whether she should run or just face whoever it was.

The crunch of leaves from her left drew her attention. No sooner had her vision shifted than a blur from the place the man had hid raced toward her. She rolled as her father had taught her to do in order to minimize the impact of the assault. At the same time, she pulled her knife and tried to put it between her and her attacker. The man grabbed her wrist and pinned it to the ground, rendering her weapon useless.

Her heart pounded in her chest and a roar sounded in her ears. Who was this man?

She fought to free herself from his hold but found he outmatched her in size, speed, and strength. In an alarmingly short span of time, she found herself pinned beneath one of the most handsome men she had ever seen. She pushed aside her shock and renewed her efforts. "Get off of me!" Even the attractiveness of his face didn't deter her from ramming her head into his nose.

He loosened his grip on her and covered his face as he mumbled some expletive.

She used this distraction to her advantage and bucked him to one side so she could wiggle free. Before she could get to her feet and scamper away, he grabbed her by the ankle.

"Let go!" She kicked at his hand with her other foot, trying to break his hold.

As she struggled with the warrior, two more men appeared from out of the surrounding trees. "Do you need help, Kajika?" the taller of the two men asked. The laughter in his tone suggested their struggle amused him.

Ahyoka renewed her efforts to break free of the first man's grip. "Who are you and what do you want?"

The warrior kept his hold of her even as he climbed to his feet. "Who are you and what were you doing in our village?"

Ahyoka stopped struggling. "In your village? What village?"

"Don't play dumb with me. We tracked you here."

"I don't know what you're talking about." She pointed to the bank just behind them. "I've been following the river all day. I stopped to rest when I realized how far I'd come. Where is your village?"

Now that he had released her, she could see the rest of the man who had interrupted her peace and quiet. Her eyes traveled up the length of his legs. She skimmed over the short deer skin he wore about his waist and tried not to speculate about what might be hidden beneath. His bow hung across his broad chest, making her wonder how he managed to squeeze into such a narrow span. Every line of his chest and belly could be seen clearly. If she wanted, she could count each one even from where she sat.

Something stirred within her and made her heart skip a beat. That same something counteracted her impulse to escape.

9

His face had neither the long, lean planes of Bodaway's tribe nor the pudgy, round cheeks of Patamon's, making it difficult to tell which of her neighboring tribes he belonged to. The feathers in his hair and the painted designs on his body marked him as an honored warrior. But even without these physical signs, she would have known based on the way he held himself, full of confidence and manly grace.

"How do we know you're telling the truth?" the warrior asked.

"How do you know I'm not?" she countered.

The tall, second man moved toward the bank. Was he looking for something?

"Where is your mate?" the warrior asked.

"I am bound to no man."

His expression wavered then turned into a frown. "What of your father or brothers? Surely one of your family is nearby waiting to escort you home."

"As you probably already know, there is no one waiting nearby." She shrugged. "I have no need of escort."

His frown deepened. "Your chief allows the unmated women in his care to wander about without a guardian or someone to watch over them?"

"Of course not. But I am not like the other women of our village."

His eyes skimmed her from head to toe. "How so? You look like a normal maiden to me. Perhaps a little thin, but not underfed."

Her cheeks grew warm. "My chief knows I can care for myself. I am allowed more freedom than most."

"So you just decided to see where the river led?" the smaller, older man asked.

"I have been collecting herbs and seeds." She shrugged. "I don't normally go this far, but the water was hard to resist today." She brushed past the warrior and returned to the place where she had been sitting. She found the bowl she'd been eating from and offered it to the men. "I don't have much, but you're welcome to refresh yourself before you continue on your way." She laid an apple and a few pieces of dried venison on the nearby grass mat then pulled another small bowl from her pouch.

"You travel alone and offer strangers your meager supplies. You either know something I do not, or you are far too trusting," the warrior said.

"Perhaps," she said, avoiding his thinly veiled question. "You have traveled some distance, have you not? Feel free to take advantage of Mother River's offerings before you go."

The warrior moved closer. "Are you in a hurry to see us leave?"

A shiver of awareness ran down her spine. Why did this man affect her so?

She handed him one of the bowls then returned to her spot on the bank. Once he had quenched his thirst, she said, "You and your fellow hunters seek something." She studied him further. "Or perhaps someone?"

There was a flash of surprise in his eye before he could hide it. "We do. What do you know of our search?"

"Only that which you have told me."

"I have told you nothing and yet you know much. How is that?"

"Ah, but you have told me much. Your markings and dress say you are warrior born and hunter charged. The silent and almost unnoticeable signals you sent the others tells me you have worked together before. And since you are here, in this quiet, secluded place instead of the hunting grounds, you must be looking for something other than food." Years of lessons learned at the hands of the suspicious and ignorant kept her silent about what the spirits had told her. "But since you're here, perhaps you could let me know who I share my resting place with?" Ahyoka asked.

"I am Kajika. We traveled from the west."

"Beyond the salt plains?"

"No."

"Yonaguska's people," she said matter-of-factly.

Kajika raised a brow. "How did you know that?"

"Reasonable guess. I know you aren't from Bodaway's village. I visited cousins there two seasons ago and didn't see any of you there. Yonaguska has the largest village this side of the salt plains, so it seems to be a safe guess."

He grunted.

"How is Winema?"

He blinked, as if surprised by her question. "Fine.

"You know Winema?" the older man asked.

"Yes." There was no reason she had to volunteer how she knew Winema.

"You haven't told us who you are," Kajika said.

"I am Ahyoka."

"And your chief is?" Kajika pressed.

"Hiamovi."

"You expect us to believe that you walked all the way here from Hiamovi's village by yourself? In less than a day?"

She shrugged. "I suspect you'll believe exactly what you want to believe."

Kajika's gaze narrowed.

"The sun will be setting. We should return, Kajika," the older man said.

Kajika stood then held his hand out to her. "Come. You will travel with us."

She looked at his outstretched palm then up into his eyes. "There is no need. I will make my own way."

"You don't understand. I cannot allow a maiden to go unescorted. There are too many dangers, but I do not have time to escort you to your village. I was sent by my chief to collect information about something that happened in our village. You are the only stranger we have come across, and he will want to ask you questions."

A death.

Mourning.

He seeks the one responsible.

Destiny.

She sighed. She hadn't planned to be gone overnight. However, Yonaguska's village was less than two day's ride away. It would be nice to visit with Winema and learn what news they had of their grandson.

She placed her hand in his. "Very well. I will go with you."

"Good." Kajika pulled her to her feet. When they were toe to toe, he added, "It wasn't really a choice."

She lifted one brow in challenge but said nothing more.

Destiny.

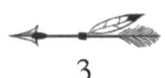

3

"Can you not sit still?" Kajika groused in Ahyoka's ear. It had been a mistake to think he could share a horse with her. Given how much Ahyoka squirmed, she had to be as uncomfortable with their closeness as him. Unfortunately, her movements were only adding to his discomfort.

"I can't help it. Something keeps digging into my hip."

"That's me," he admitted through gritted teeth.

She froze. He couldn't see her entire face, but her cheeks became stained pink and her eyes widened.

Since they hadn't known how long they would be gone, they had packed extra supplies. Those supplies were tied to the back of each of the horses, leaving no room for an extra passenger. Riding with one of the others had simply not been an option as far as Kajika was concerned.

"How much farther?" she asked.

"You don't know?" He wanted to believe she did not know where the village was, but his determination to find Dyami's killer ran hot.

She shook her head. "No. I've never been to your village."

"You hinted you knew Yonaguska and where the village was."

"I know Winema better. She told me where your village was."

"How do you know them but have never been to our village? They rarely travel."

She took a deep breath, as if annoyed by his questions. "I met them a few turns of the moon ago in Avonaco's village."

Yonaguska and Winema had traveled north to visit their eldest daughter, Luyo, when she gave birth. Ahyoka could be telling the truth. But how likely could that be? The trail the killer had left led them to Ahyoka.

His gut told him she hid something. If she lied to protect the guilty party, he would not go easy on her later. Her pretty face would not deter him from finding who was responsible for what happened to his cousin and his family. They deserved no less.

If Ahyoka was involved, perhaps Winema would be able to whittle the truth out of her. His stomach clenched at the thought of what he might be forced to do if it fell to him to get her to talk.

"Is that it?"

Her question jerked him out of his thoughts. A small poof of smoke in the distance was the only hint of settlement. Even the path they followed wasn't worn enough to be noticeable to most.

"Yes. How did you know?"

She shrugged. "Just hoping, really."

"Tired of me already?" For some reason the thought that she might be did not sit well with him.

"No." She quickly added, "But your poor horse is probably tired from carrying both of us and it is getting uncomfortable riding this way."

"Yes, it is," he agreed. He tried to shift them to give her a little more room, but all he succeeded in doing was sliding her rear across his already uncomfortable erection.

As they neared the village, he waved Yansa forward. "Ride ahead and notify Yonaguska of our return." He motioned to Ahyoka with a slight tip of his head. "And let him know we're bringing someone for him to speak with."

Yansa grunted in acknowledgement then kicked his horse into a run.

When Kajika and Neka reached the entrance to their village, they were greeted by a small assembly. Others stood at the openings of their tepees, perhaps hoping for a glimpse at the one who may have been responsible for bringing fear to their homes.

In front of him, Ahyoka tensed even more.

Did she fear being recognized? Or that she might be exposed as a liar? Disappointment washed through him, just when he had begun to hope she wasn't involved in Ghigau's death.

He spotted Yonaguska outside of the main tepee. Several

warriors and braves flanked the chief.

Kajika directed his horse to the boy waiting to help. He handed the reins down then swung his leg around and dismounted. He reached for Ahyoka to help her slide from the saddle. Once her feet were firmly on the ground, he took her arm and steered her to where the chief waited. He gave her no opportunity to flee.

He greeted the chief then nodded to Ahyoka. "I understand you already know Ahyoka?"

The chief glanced at her. "Yes," he said with a brisk nod. "We met while visiting Luyo. Why has she been brought here?"

"We found her along the river and I—"

"Ahyoka? Is that you?" Winema asked as she exited the tepee.

Ahyoka shot Kajika an I-told-you-so look then smiled warmly at the plump older woman. "Winema." She moved toward Winema. "It is good to see you again."

Winema pulled Ahyoka into a hug that could easily have smothered the younger woman. While still holding Ahyoka by the arms, she asked, "Did you receive our gifts?"

"I did. Thank you for your generosity."

They sent gifts to Ahyoka? Kajika mentally kicked himself.

Ahyoka turned toward the chief. "My brother very much appreciated the arrows. It took almost a full turn of the moon before he mastered how to shoot them. Even longer to make them."

Yonaguska chuckled.

"Come, there is much to catch up on." Winema pulled Ahyoka toward the tepee entrance then stopped and looked back. "Unless you need her for something?"

Yonaguska raised one brow and looked at Kajika.

"We will find her if we need her," he assured them.

Winema tugged Ahyoka through the opening of the tepee, chattering all the while.

"Tell me," the chief said when they were alone again.

Kajika took a deep breath. "Perhaps we should get comfortable?"

Yonaguska grunted his assent and led the way to the gathering place. The warriors and braves who had been standing nearby dispersed as the chief took his usual seat.

Kajika told him of the previous two day's travels and everything he had learned, or more specifically not learned, from Ahyoka.

When he'd finished, Yonaguska leaned back and folded his arms across his chest.

"Do you know what she is?" Yonaguska asked.

"What do you mean?"

"That girl, that woman," he indicated the tepee Winema had pulled Ahyoka into with a jerk of his chin, "is unlike any you will ever meet."

Kajika contained his disbelief.

"She is what the elders call a spirit talker."

"A spirit talker," Kajika said without asking the obvious question.

"She has the ability to hear spirits in everything around us. It's been said that she hears the voices of the animals, the trees, water, and even the land itself."

"Voices." How could his own chief expect him to believe this?

Yonaguska leaned forward and rested his elbows on his knees. "Any medicine man will tell you that every living thing or being has a life force. A spirit, if you will. And like us, everything communicates in some way. But not all of us have been blessed to understand."

"But she can." He held his tongue. Yonaguska knew well what he thought about medicine men and their so-called beliefs.

Yonaguska nodded.

"How do you know she is what you say?"

"Her birth was foretold by the elders. And since then we have watched. She has done some amazing things in her young life." He looked Kajika in the eye. "Including saving the life of my daughter and grandson."

A weight settled in Kajika's stomach.

"I'm sure you've heard the stories already. It was a difficult birth. The baby was stuck and Luyo was bleeding too much. If Ahyoka had not been there, we would have lost them both." He rubbed his forehead. "She said the spirits of our ancestors who protect the land guided her to Luyo's village because it was important that the baby be born." He looked to Kajika. "I don't care about why or how she came to be there, I'm just glad she was."

Wild animals, a trail that could be followed, even a scent on the wind. These things were familiar. These things he understood. Spirits and shadows and things he couldn't touch disturbed him.

"So the spirits tell her things?"

"Apparently."

"What kind of things?"

"I don't know." Once more he gestured to the tepee. "Winema could tell you more. She and Ahyoka spent many days together." With a meaningful look, he added, "She is quite devoted to Ahyoka. I recommend you don't do anything to insult or hurt her."

"I would never intentionally harm an honored guest."

"I know. But women are sensitive and, according to Winema, Ahyoka is particularly so with regard to her abilities."

Kajika frowned. "In what way?"

"Apparently she has few friends and is often shunned. Many in her own village avoid her because they can't make up their mind about whether she is a liar or just crazy."

Anger swelled within Kajika. He'd seen firsthand just how cruel people could be. His own mother had been shunned by her family because she had chosen his father instead of someone from her own village as husband.

"As you've probably already learned, she's reluctant to tell people what she hears and what she knows."

"Do you think she knows what happened to Ghigau?"

"If she doesn't, she may be able to find out."

"Would she tell us if she did?"

Yonaguska shrugged. "If she trusts you she may."

"Would she tell Winema?"

"I expect Winema is already learning what she can. In between baby stories, that is." He tapped his finger on the log he leaned against. "Do you want her to question Ahyoka for you?"

"No."

"I thought not." Yonaguska's gaze turned thoughtful. "If you expect her to open up to you and help find the killer, you'll have to earn her trust. Can you do that?"

Kajika folded his arms across his chest. "I can try."

"It's going to take more than a little effort on your part, you know." Yonaguska leaned in his direction. "I'm afraid this may be one of those times where you are going to end up needing to trust yourself as well as her and open your heart and mind to things that are not of the world we see around us."

"So you believe she talks to spirits?"

"I believe there are things in this world we do not understand.

Things we cannot see, hear, or touch and yet they are there. I believe she has gifts. She has proven that more than once. But I do not know the extent of them." Yonaguska gave him an odd look. "It might be helpful for you to find out."

Kajika's frown deepened. He had been relieved to learn Ahyoka told the truth about knowing Yonaguska and Winema. Hopefully that meant she wasn't hiding anything about Ghigau's death.

But that didn't mean he readily believed she could talk to spirits.

4

She'd tried. After tossing and turning and even covering her head with a fur, Ahyoka still couldn't sleep.

Chief Yonaguska's snores echoed around the sizable tepee. How did Winema sleep next to him every night and remain sane?

There was still some time before dawn. Since she couldn't sleep, she might as well use the privacy of the night to speak to the spirits of the village and learn what she could about the killings. After Winema told her what had happened to that woman and her child, she felt compelled to help however she could.

She tiptoed out of the tepee to avoid waking Winema or the chief. As she stood outside in the cooler night air, she reached out with her senses. Winema told her there was a small pond east of the village. That would be the most likely place for animals and insects to gather.

The people of the village may not have seen anything when Ghigau had been killed, but the creatures in the area would have picked up smells, sounds, and high emotions.

Following a trail only she could see in the dark, Ahyoka made her way to the pond. She passed the spirit of more than one of Kajika's ancestors, but she avoided contact with them. She didn't know what Ghigau looked like, so there was little point looking for her spirit—if she still remained. Given the level of violence that had so recently occurred, it would probably be better to start with the land and the animals.

Come, Spirit Talker.

We greet you.
Come.
We play in the moonlight.
Come.
Brother Fox waits.

The warmth of the land reached up to her. It flowed through the soles of her bare feet and tickled her toes. A family of bats circled overhead and called out their greeting. Bugs she couldn't see clearly scattered underfoot. A coyote mother cried in the distance. Her cubs yipped in response.

When she reached the edge of the pond, she gazed at the moon reflected in the water's surface. In tribute to the Moon Goddess, she raised her hands above her head and murmured the words her mother had taught her years before.

In response, a welcoming breeze rippled through her hair, cooling her skin.

She smiled, accepting the blessing, and reached for the laces of her dress. Once the closure was loose enough, she pulled her dress over her head and dropped it on the ground, away from the water's edge.

Slowly she made her way into the water. When it reached her lower back, she sank below the surface. Her ears were filled with greetings from the fish and turtles.

When she came up for air, the welcoming sounds that had been there before were all but silent.

The hunter.
He came.
The hunter.
He watches.

Keeping most of her body below the surface, she scanned the bank and the surrounding area.

Kajika.

Why had he followed her? How long had he been there? Her cheeks heated in embarrassment, wondering how long he'd been there. Her clothes were on the bank, several feet away from the water's edge. He would see her when she climbed out.

Her heart skipped a beat. She was out here alone with an unmated man. Presumably no one in the village knew they were here. Anything could happen and no one would be the wiser.

Winema had told her that Kajika was one of Yonaguska's most

trusted warriors. If his intentions were sinister or he meant her harm, the spirits would warn her. For now they were silent. Perhaps they too waited to see what would happen.

What did she want to happen?

She could call out and demand he return to the village and give her privacy. She could also pretend he was not there and carry on with her own business. But Kajika was a hard man to ignore. Especially here, in the still of the night. His spirit radiated like a beacon to her.

Destiny.

Her breath stalled in her throat. Had she finally met her one? If she had, there would be no point in fighting the pull between them. The spirits decreed he was somehow tied to her destiny. She just needed to figure out how.

Coming to her full height, she stood proudly in the light of the full moon. Once she squeezed the water from her hair, she headed to the shoreline to retrieve her clothing. Winema had offered her a change of clothing and now that she had rinsed the day's dust and sweat from her body, she regretted not taking the offer of a clean dress. Perhaps after the sun had risen she would take Winema's offer, but for now, her own would have to do.

After securing the laces on her dress she knelt, facing the pond and the night sky. She scanned the area with her senses and found Kajika had moved closer yet remained hidden.

She calmed her skittish heart and prepared to open herself to the spirits of the land and the sky. The walls she had built over the years to block out the bombardment of voices were sturdy. Years of practice allowed her to open the floodgates with relative ease.

When she did, a blanket of light rippled across the plains that lay beyond the pond. The essence from souls long departed from the mortal world appeared, both man and beast. They floated like fireflies above the tall grass.

The birds, animals, and insects that still lived radiated with golden flames.

Voices bombarded her from all sides.

Some called out to the Moon Goddess, others prayed to the Great Spirit.

One voice rose above the rest. *Welcome sister.*

Ahyoka turned in the direction of the voice. A large male fox trotted in her direction. His spirit glowed with an inner flame that lent him an ethereal quality.

She dipped her head in respect. "Brother Fox."

We are honored by your visit.

"Thank you."

You come at a disturbing time. Death walks our land.

"The family in the village. I would like to help, but I don't know where to start. Do you know what form death takes?"

Many.

Ahyoka frowned. "The villagers are frightened. They believe an animal is responsible."

They search for truth in the wrong places.

"Where should they look?"

Within.

Her frown deepened. Perhaps someone within the village was guilty? "How can I help the woman and her child find peace?"

The fox looked to the fields where most of the spirit lights floated. *That will be difficult. They are trapped between worlds.*

Her breath caught. There were very few things that could trap a person's spirit between worlds and none of them were good. "What keeps them from moving on?"

Their spirits were drained before they could cross over.

Ahyoka's soul chilled. "What of her husband?"

He is trapped as well.

"For the same reason?"

Yes.

"So he wasn't responsible for their deaths."

No. The fox's eyes took on another level of sadness. *Even now he searches for them.*

"They are not together?"

No.

Her heart ached for them. "What about the child?"

The child's spirit was too closely linked to his mother to be severed even by this evil.

She said a prayer of thanks. "If I find the one who drained their spirits, can they make their final journey? Together?"

Yes. But only if their spirits are freed before they fade completely.

"How much time do I have?" Once a spirit faded, they would not be able to cross into the Great Hunting Grounds. They would forever be trapped between worlds. And obviously, they would not be together.

Not long. Perhaps until the new moon.

"I will find the one responsible."

Take care, Spirit Talker. I have not felt this kind of evil for some time.

"I will."

The fox looked to where Kajika hid. *The warrior doesn't believe as you do.*

Her eyes darted to the same spot.

You must help him see with eyes that may never be opened.

"I will try."

The fox stood to leave. *The other spirits and I will do what we can to help you cleanse our lands of this evil.*

"Thank you."

Sister rabbit said if you send men with their dogs to the north, where the path leads into the trees, you will find the one that is missing.

She dipped her head. "I will tell the chief."

May the Great Spirit's blessings be upon you, Spirit Talker.

"And you, Brother Fox."

With a yip, the sleek creature sprinted into the tall grass and disappeared from her sight.

She took a cleansing breath. Kajika needed to know what she had learned.

Would he listen to the things she needed to tell him? And if he did, what would he think of her afterward? Would he make fun of her? Or worse, say that she was out of her head and dismiss her all together?

She shuddered.

She'd just have to figure out another way of revealing what she had learned.

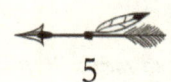

5

Kajika switched his weight from one leg to the other to ease some of the tension. At least his rock-hard erection had returned to the semi-hard state it had been in ever since meeting Ahyoka. When she came out of the pond wearing nothing but moonlight, he had to fight his instinct to carry her to his tepee and not let her out until they were both too tired to move.

For a moment, he forgot that she was an honored guest of his chief. Even his uncertainty over whether she had something to do with Ghigau's death had been pushed to the back of his mind. It didn't matter that she was from an eastern tribe. And if she could hear animals speaking to her, he didn't care.

Not right then. Not in that moment.

There was one thing that kept him from marching up to her and verifying if the interest he thought he had seen in her eyes earlier that day had been real or imagined. What if she was a maiden? Untouched by any man. If so, then he had no right to press her. That alone stopped him in his tracks.

Yet that same thought made him burn for her. He wanted to caress every womanly curve he had seen against the backdrop of the night. He wanted to lick each and every drop of water from her skin then immerse her again so he could start all over.

He strongly suspected that touching her would be like reaching for lightening.

Even if he didn't burn up, he would never be the same.

Visions of her naked body distracted him, making it hard to

focus on what she was doing.

Her voice carried across the field, but he couldn't see anyone with her. With nothing to shield him from view, he didn't dare move closer. But it would have been impossible for anyone to approach without him noticing.

Perhaps she talked to herself.

Or to spirits?

He frowned. Just because she talked to them didn't mean they talked back.

The breeze rippled through the grass surrounding him, catching his attention. Ahyoka stood and walked in his direction. He flattened himself against the ground, hoping she wouldn't see him. To his amazement, she stopped just in front of him and asked, "Are you going to stay out here all night or do you want to walk back to the village with me?"

Kajika allowed his gaze to roam across her bare feet, up her legs to the bottom edge of her dress. He lingered near her hips then traveled up as high as he could without straining his neck. Finally, he rolled to the side then came to his full standing height.

"What are you doing out here alone?" he demanded.

"I'm not alone."

He looked around the field. "Who else is with you?"

"You."

"I know, but you didn't know I was here."

"Yes, I did."

He frowned. "How?"

She tugged at his arm and tried to turn him in the direction of the village. "Walk with me and I will tell you."

"Why? Is there someone else here and you're trying to help them slip away unnoticed?"

She dropped her hand, making him instantly regret his words. "No. But since you have no reason to believe me, I can show you where I knelt near the water. You can look at the tracks."

He wanted to believe her, but experience had taught him to doubt. He finally grumbled, "That won't be necessary."

She studied his face, as he had hers. "Shall we move on then?"

He narrowed his gaze. Did she mean their walk back to the village or their dealings with each other? Either way, it felt as if they stood at some crossroad. "Yes. Perhaps we should."

She picked her way around rocks and stumps and other

obstacles as she walked. It was odd how she seemed to be able to see clearly in the dark. Even with the nearly full moon, he had to tread carefully so as to not stumble.

"Are you going to tell me what you were doing out here alone?" he asked again.

"Do you want the easy answer or the hard one?"

He reached for her arm and pulled her to a stop. "I want the truth."

"Very well." She resumed her walk. "Initially I needed some air because I couldn't sleep." She gave him a sheepish smile. "Chief Yonaguska snores more than a grizzly."

Kajika grunted in assent. He'd been subjected to the chief's snores more than once on hunting trips.

"It felt so nice outside that I decided to walk around."

"At night? Why? You can't see anything."

She stopped and turned to face him. "Are you a praying man, Kajika?"

He swallowed his initial answer. Normally he would have given her an earful about how useless prayers were, but he didn't want to insult her. He needed to earn her trust, so a lie wouldn't do either. "No. Not for a very long time."

"But you used to be."

He turned away, resuming their walk back to the village. "Yes."

"Well, some of us enjoy the peace and quiet the night brings and use those moments to seek guidance from beyond this world."

"Are you telling me that you were praying?"

She pushed a low hanging limb out of her way. "I was listening."

"To what?"

"To everything."

"And what did you learn?"

"That whoever killed your cousin and his family took their…" She struggled to find a word to fit what she needed to explain. "The essence—the fuel—that makes up their spirits. Without it, their spirits cannot make their way to the Great Hunting Grounds."

Kajika grabbed her arm once again and came to a halt. "Dyami is dead? How do you know?"

"I, uh…"

"No one has seen him. How do you know he is dead?" He

tugged her closer. "And do not lie."

"I just do."

He searched her expression but found nothing to make him think she lied. "Then where is he?"

She bit her lip.

"Tell me!"

"I believe if your men took their dogs to the north, where the path leads into the trees, they will find what you are looking for."

He tightened his grip on her arm. "How do you know this?"

She held his gaze. "Do not ask me questions you do not want the answers to."

They had a silent battle of wills before he finally released her. They resumed their walk back to the village.

"I'm sorry for your loss, Kajika."

"What if I choose to not believe you?"

She shrugged. "It will make what I have to do harder, but eventually the truth will come out."

"And just what do you have to do?"

"I have to find whoever killed your cousin and his family before the new moon."

"Why? What happens at the new moon?" he asked, already dreading the answer.

"If I don't, their spirits will wither and die and they will never be able to cross into the Great Hunting Grounds." If possible, her eyes turned even more sad. "And the three of them will spend eternity lost and apart."

He wanted to scoff at what she said, but something buried deep within him cried out in warning. What if what she said was true? Ghigau had been a spiritual woman. Dyami had often spoken fondly of the Great Hunting Grounds and how he looked forward to hunting with his ancestors. Could he be risking Dyami and Ghigau and the baby's afterlife?

"No," Kajika said flatly.

"No, what?"

He cut off those thoughts and pointed at her. "You are not going to find the man or the thing that did this. I was tasked by my chief to find out what happened and bring justice and peace back to our village. And that is exactly what I will do."

"Do you think you can find them on your own?" she demanded.

"That's what I was doing until we ran into you."

"Are you saying it's my fault that you stopped your hunt?"

"The trail led us right to you. Yonaguska told us he wanted to question anyone we found."

"I see." She lifted her chin. "And what will you do when you find the one responsible for your cousin's death?"

"That depends. If it turns out that an animal was responsible, I will make sure it fills someone's soup pot before it harms anyone else. If I find a man responsible, I would be under oath to bring them before my chief so that fair punishment could be passed upon them." He held up one finger. "However..." A muscle jumped in his jaw. "If they attacked me or my men, I would not hesitate to protect myself. No matter the cost."

He glanced toward the horizon where the sun had turned into streaks of pink and orange. "You must return to Yonaguska's tepee. The village will wake soon, and I must think about what you have said." He took a deep breath. "And I must decide how much to tell Yonaguska."

"Perhaps it would be best to see if your men are able to find your cousin's body?"

"How do I explain sending them to a particular location?"

"The chief would not be surprised by my knowing something that no one else would." She made a harrumphing sound. "I suspect that he would be more surprised that you believed me enough to follow my advice."

"I didn't say I believed you, but I see little harm in checking where you say. At most it would waste a bit of the men's day." He shrugged. "It would do the dogs some good to get out and look for a trail."

She flinched, making him regret his words. "Thank you for telling me about Dyami. I may not believe everything you've said but, as Yonaguska often tells me, we don't know everything there is to know about our world. I may need to see, hear, or touch something before I believe in it, but I am willing to leave room for the possibility."

She inclined her head. "That is all I will ask." She raised her eyes to meet his. "For now."

With a timid smile, she stepped around him and headed to the chief's tepee.

6

Ahyoka hadn't been gone long before the first of the young braves arrived to tend to the horses. Kajika dallied for a bit, hoping one of his fellow hunters would rise early. Finally, he left word with one of the men to have a small hunting party sent out to the north, as Ahyoka had said, and then he too went to get some sleep.

The sun was high in the sky when he left his tepee.

After bartering with one of the widows for his lunch, he went in search of Yonaguska. He found the chief at the gathering place discussing the matters of the day with his advisors. When Kajika approached, the chief waved him forward.

"Sleep well?" There was a hint of a smirk when Yonaguska asked.

"I did." He took in the number of people gathered around them. "What have I missed?"

Yonaguska grunted and waved his question away. "Just dealing with the usual complaints. This one needs more meat. That one more grain. I should make one of the braves who claim to want to be in charge listen to these women all day." He laughed. "That would cure them of some of their know-it-all attitude."

"That it would."

Yonaguska's face turned serious. "Just after first meal, Galegenoh and his sons gathered a few of the dogs and headed to the north. They said it was on your orders. Care to tell me what that was about?"

"Actually, it was due to something Ahyoka told me. I thought it wouldn't hurt to find out what happened if I followed her suggestion."

"A test of sorts?"

"I suppose you could say that."

"Do I need to tell you how I'd have wagered?"

Kajika shrugged. "That won't be necessary." The area was too crowded to tell him everything Ahyoka had said, so he remained silent about their spirits. "Any word from Galegenoh?"

"No." The chief looked to the north. "I admit, I expected them to be back by now." He looked to Kajika. "Should I be worried?"

"I don't think so, but Ahyoka would be the one to ask."

"She went with the women down to the river to wash clothes and gather flowers or whatever it is that women do."

An image of Ahyoka standing in the full moon light with drops of water running down her naked body flashed into his mind. He struggled to control the erection that threatened to pop up and embarrass him.

Why did this woman affect him so?

There was a maiden in his village whose father had made it perfectly clear that, if he were to choose her for a bride, his interest would be welcomed. The maiden had a pretty face but didn't captivate him the way Ahyoka had. Even the widow who occasionally warmed his bed didn't stir his blood so.

He shook his head. Ahyoka was becoming a distraction, one he needed to get away from. But the idea that he was running away rankled. He wasn't a coward. He had always faced challenges head on. Win or lose. Why should she be any different?

He rose to his feet.

"I don't know where you're going, but do I need to send someone with you?" The chief's question cut into his thoughts.

"Why would you send someone with me?"

"Because the look on your face could drop a grizzly at a hundred paces."

"What are you talking about?"

The chief pointed at him. "You look angry enough to take on a charging bear. What were you thinking about?"

Kajika scrubbed his hand over his face. "I don't know what I was thinking."

Yonaguska studied him. "Which woman has you so mixed up? Surely not that young maiden that Ohanko has been pushing your way?"

"Definitely not her." He rubbed his temple. "I mean, no. No one has me mixed up, as you put it."

"Only a woman could have this kind of effect on a man."

"Do we really need to discuss this right now?" He looked at the group of men around them. Several wore expressions of sympathy. The older men grinned.

The chief chuckled. "Fine." Then his amusement melted away. "Looks like we really will need to discuss this later."

Kajika turned to see what had caught Yonaguska's attention.

Galegenoh and his sons had just entered the village. One of the horses pulled a makeshift sled. A sled large enough to hold a body. Whatever they returned with had been covered by skins.

That was never a good sign.

Kajika and the others came to their feet as Galegenoh dismounted from his horse.

He made the proper greetings to the chief and the elders, then turned to look at Kajika. "You were right. The dogs picked up the scent before we even made it to the tree line."

"What took so long?" Chief asked.

"We, uh…" Galegenoh glanced at Kajika. "We had trouble getting the body out."

"Out? Out of what?" Kajika stepped forward.

Galegenoh lowered his voice. "A hollowed-out tree that was partially buried underground."

Kajika frowned in confusion. "How did he get in there?"

Galegenoh shook his head. "Someone had to have put him there. I've never seen an animal do that sort of thing."

"Take him to Ituha so he can be readied for burial," Yonaguska said with a meaningful glance at the people who were coming out to look. "We'll talk about the details later."

They quickly dispersed. Galegenoh led the horse pulling Dyami's body to Ituha's hut while his sons took the dogs to be fed and watered. Yonaguska left with two of the elders. Kajika headed toward Yonaguska and Winema's tepee before he realized where he was going.

Obviously Ahyoka had been right. But how did she know? She said she had been listening. But to what? The wind? An animal couldn't have told her where to find Dyami. That just didn't happen. Perhaps she saw animals in that area acting strange,

31

making her believe someone or something was buried there.

He shook his head.

As far as he knew, she hadn't been to the place where Dyami was found. She rode in with him from the east then spent the evening with Winema in their tepee. When she left the village to go to the pond, he had followed.

Unless Ahyoka had been involved with the killings, he had no explanation for how she knew where to find Dyami.

"Your face is going to stay like that if you're not careful."

Ahyoka's statement startled him out of his thoughts. "Like what?"

She tilted her head to one side and gestured at his face. "It looks like you tasted something foul and are really angry about it."

He grunted then shrugged. "I suppose that's close enough to the truth." After folding his arms across his chest, he looked down at her. "Where were you headed?"

"We heard the men had returned with a body. I was coming to find out if it was your cousin."

"I haven't seen the body to know for certain, but Galegenoh acted as if it were Dyami. Why?"

"I was going to ask Chief Yonaguska if I could see Dyami before they prepare him."

He was taken back. "Why would you want to do that?"

"There are a great many things you can tell about how a person spent their last moments before death if you just look."

Kajika shuddered with distaste. "If you're going to, you had best hurry. They're taking him to Ituha now."

"Is that the person who will make the burial preparations?"

"Yes," he nodded.

"Then yes, I best hurry." She started to turn away then paused. "I don't suppose you know where Yonaguska is, do you?"

He turned and pointed to where he had last seen the large man. "He was with a couple of the elders reviewing the day's issues, but he may have gone to tell Winema what happened."

Ahyoka shook her head. "I just left her and I didn't pass him along the way."

He took a deep breath to resign himself to the idea of spending time with her, despite how uncomfortable she made him. "Come. I will help you find him."

"You don't need to do that. Really." She waved her hand. "I

can find him on my own."

"I'm sure you can, but I may as well come along." He grumbled, "It'll probably be less frustrating for me in the long run."

7

The fluttery sensations she had experienced yesterday came back as soon as she saw Kajika in the village. Despite his gruff demeanor, she had seen enough to know he had a caring soul. And those eyes of his drank in everything and quickly turned it into usable information.

But it was his broad shoulders and muscular chest that captivated her.

During the ride to his village, she had to remind herself more than once that it wouldn't be acceptable to pet him. Especially since she hadn't known at the time if he had a wife. Now that she knew he didn't, the temptation had only grown. Her fear that he might think her odd kept her in check.

Shaking off her depressing thoughts, she followed Kajika through the village until they found Chief Yonaguska. The chief agreed to let her look at Dyami's body but suggested it might be best to do it while Ituha, the elder who would be handling the burial, gathered the supplies he needed. That would raise fewer questions from the villagers and wouldn't interrupt the burial ceremony.

Kajika led her to a structure on the far edge of the village. The hut had been made from cut trees, similar to dwellings the settlers lived in. The sturdy materials probably provided better protection from the weather and animals.

The men who brought Dyami home had left him on their makeshift sled beneath the animal skins. A knot formed in her throat when she saw the outline of the body. Despite years of training as a healer, she disliked disturbing the dead. If his body had been left several days ago, it would have started to decay. She hesitated near the door.

"You don't have to do this," Kajika told her softly.

She smiled at him for his thoughtfulness. "I was just about to tell you the same thing."

"I'll be fine." His lips were pressed into a firm line.

"Let's see what we're dealing with." She moved closer to the body. When she was only a few feet away, a feeling of dread and malice swept over her skin. She reached for Kajika. "Don't touch him."

"Why not?"

"Something evil did this."

"I'm sure they were, but we need to know it's Dyami for certain."

She tightened her grip on his arm. "I don't mean just bad or mean or sinful. I mean…" She gestured to her own chest. "True evil." She choked down the need to vomit. "And it's powerful." She looked up into his eyes. "Do you not sense something? Something that makes you want to turn away from what you see before you?"

"Yes. But there's nothing unusual about not wanting to see the dead." He glanced at Dyami's body. "Especially when it's someone you knew and cared for."

"There's more to it." She drew on her gift that allowed her to see spirits and studied Dyami's covered form.

"What are you doing?" Kajika took a step back.

"I just… I am going to make sure there is nothing harmful to us before we touch anything."

"Why did your eyes change into a fiery gold?"

She grimaced. Most people feared her gifts. When they saw evidence of them at work, their fears often intensified. "I…" She ducked her head. "I needed to better see what we might be dealing with."

"Interesting," he mumbled.

Using a stick she found lying next to the hut, she lifted the edge of the skins covering Dyami. "I think it will be okay to touch the skins covering him." She banked her gift before looking up at him. "But if I tell you to stop or not touch something, please know it's for your own good."

He frowned but finally nodded. "Very well." He squatted next to the sled then lifted the coverings up and away from the body.

Ahyoka swallowed and fought the ill feelings rolling through her belly.

Kajika mumbled an expletive.

Dirt covered Dyami's body from head to foot. His deerskin pants were stained with blood. Her gifts told her the blood on Dyami's clothes came from Ghigau and the child. She fought her natural inclination to turn away from the gruesome sight in order to learn what she could about the killer.

Dyami had been cut from the center of his ribs to below the waist of his breeches. While she didn't know what he normally looked like, she could tell the bruises from the beating he had taken had distorted his face. In addition to the big one down the center, there were small cuts and scrapes all over his chest.

"It does look like he got into a fight with some kind of wild animal," Kajika said.

"To most people probably."

He looked up at her. "But not you?"

"Too much evil clings to his body for this to simply be a wild animal. I sense malicious intent, a need for vengeance and a lust for power." She moved toward Dyami's feet to look from a different angle. She frowned. "His insides were removed."

Kajika whipped his head around to study Dyami's belly. He reached to touch.

"Don't." Her warning stopped him just in time. She handed him the stick she had used. "Don't touch him with your bare hands."

Thankfully he didn't argue, nor did he question what she had told him. He used the twig to press the cut in Dyami's belly open. "You're right. They are gone." He sat back on his haunches. "An animal couldn't have done that without ripping him open." The muscle in his jaw tensed. Through gritted teeth he asked, "Why would someone do this?"

She chewed her lip. "I have an idea, but it's nothing I want to repeat unless I am certain. Unfortunately, I have heard of people, and even animals, being killed like this before."

"Tell me," he demanded as he rose to his feet.

She checked to make sure they were still alone. "I've heard

stories of shaman who are able to assume the form of animals. They are able to do it using magic and by wearing the animal's skin."

He frowned and gestured to Dyami's body. "What does that have to do with him?"

"I'm wondering if someone killed Dyami and then assumed his form to enter the village."

Kajika's quick intake of breath hinted he had heard what she'd said.

She continued with her theory. "It would explain how no one noticed a stranger in the village or why Ghigau didn't cry out. If she believed Dyami had come home, she would have no reason to raise an alarm."

"That isn't possible," he muttered through clenched teeth.

"From what I've been taught, yes, it is possible. I just don't know why someone would do it."

He paced away from her, shaking his head. "No."

She flinched. People rarely believed her, but she had hoped he might be one of the few who did. "I know you don't believe me, and I'd really like to be wrong about this." She took a step in his direction. "But I don't think that I am. Everything I see here tells me there is something evil about this killing. And I need to find out what it is."

His head whipped around. "Why?" He moved toward her. "He's my cousin. I will avenge them. I will give them the peace they need to make it to the Great Hunting Grounds."

Despite his hostile stance, she held her ground. "Because you brought me here and dropped me in the middle of this. Brother Fox said I would be needed to find the one responsible, so I will stay until they are found. There are things going on here that are beyond your skill. Bows and arrows will only do so much against someone skilled with dark magic."

He took a step closer. "You assume that I believe in that sort of thing."

"That's exactly why you're going to need my help."

He shook his head and looked down at Dyami. After taking a deep breath, the fight seemed to drain out of him. "He didn't look like that in life. Usually he was the upbeat one. Always making jests and teasing the young ones. And he loved Ghigau and the baby. More than life itself." He raised pain-filled eyes to hers. "He couldn't have killed her. He would have given his own life before he let anything happen to them."

"He may have," she told him quietly. "You can tell he put up quite a fight. And if what you say is true, whoever did this probably went through him to get to Ghigau and the baby. Which makes me wonder why. Why go through all of this trouble for a woman and a child? What was so special about them?"

She quickly added, "Not to say they weren't special to Dyami or to your village. But why would someone want to kill the two of them? Out of an entire village of people?"

Kajika turned thoughtful. "You said the fuel of their spirits had been taken."

"That's right."

"Would a shaman's spirit be any different than others?"

"Yes, actually, most of them do have stronger, more vivid spirits than other people. Why?"

"Ghigau came from another village. One from the western lands. Dyami met her on one of his trading trips. He told me not long after they were joined that she was the illegitimate daughter of a very powerful shaman. Supposedly, she had visions of the future. What if she were killed because of who her father was?"

"It's possible." She drew out the words. If she and the baby were killed because of their magnified spirits, the person who did it would not be easy to find or bring to justice. And that person would not give up the claimed spirits without a fight. Bringing peace to Dyami, Ghigau, and their baby in the spirit world would not be a simple task.

"We should talk to Yonaguska before Ituha returns," he said, interrupting her thoughts.

"Yes, we should."

Kajika covered Dyami with the skins, then took her arm to lead her away.

As they walked toward the center of the village, Ahyoka broached an idea that had been brewing in the back of her mind. "Have they done anything with Dyami and Ghigau's tepee yet?"

"I don't know."

"Would anyone be offended if I were to look around?"

"My initial reaction is to tell you no, that you don't need to see that, but I suspect it would be pointless. We can ask Yonaguska." He grunted. "Perhaps Winema would be the better leader to ask.

She would know what the busybodies of the village would consider a breach of respect."

"Busybodies?"

"The old women"—he shrugged—"and sometimes men, who have nothing better to do than talk about what everyone in the village is doing and what they should or shouldn't be doing."

"Every village has them, I'm afraid." Her gaze turned distant as she remembered more than one run-in with such people. "They can be vicious sometimes."

"Yes, they can," he murmured.

"Winema would know best. I agree we should ask her."

They walked in silence until they found Yonaguska. Luckily, he and Winema were having a meal together. The chief's tepee provided enough privacy for Ahyoka to share what they learned and to make her request.

"So you can see things about people's spirits? Not just spirits of the dead? I wondered about that." Winema leaned closer. "What do they look like? What does mine look like? And Yonaguska's."

Ahyoka looked wide-eyed at Kajika, hoping he would say something to help. His expression was unreadable, but she could tell there would be no help from him.

Yonaguska spoke up instead. "Perhaps you should save your questions for another time. It sounds as if Ahyoka has a few things she needs to take care of in a short amount of time." He looked from Ahyoka to Kajika and back again. "Especially if you are planning to take her back to her village before her father comes looking for her."

She faced Kajika. "I do need to return soon. I need to tell Hiamovi what has happened." To Winema she added, "And I need to tell him of the dream I had."

"What dream?" Kajika asked.

"We could send a messenger," Winema suggested, ignoring Kajika's question.

"I'm not sure it's safe for anyone to travel alone," Ahyoka protested. "My news will just have to wait until I return home."

"Very well," Yonaguska said, and he poured himself a fresh glass of water. "Do what you must. I'll leave it to Winema to decide if anyone would be offended if you were to enter Dyami's tepee."

"I think if you do it quickly and quietly, I doubt anyone will even notice." Winema waved her spoon at Kajika. "If you are with her, people are likely to think you are gathering personal items for Dyami's burial."

Kajika nodded his agreement.

"Thank you," Ahyoka said. "Perhaps we'll find something helpful."

"I certainly hope so," Yonaguska said. "I need to be able to tell our people something. Each of their deaths could be passed off as an animal attack based on how they look. But separate animal attacks on the same family on the same day in two different locations is a little hard to swallow."

"Agreed," Kajika said as he stood.

"We'll expect you for the evening meal." Winema looked at both of them meaningfully.

"But find me if you learn anything before then," Yonaguska added as Kajika and Ahyoka stepped to the exit.

Once they were outside, Kajika asked again, "What dream were you talking about?"

8

For some reason, he insisted on hearing about her dream. She'd tried to brush him off more than once, but he didn't give in. She finally admitted, "I think it was a warning about trouble heading toward my village."

"What kind of trouble?"

She shook her head. "I'm not certain. I couldn't see what was behind me."

He grabbed her arm and pulled her to a stop. "What could you see?"

"You."

"Me?" He took a step back. "You think I'm bringing trouble to your village?"

"No."

He crossed his arms over his chest. "Explain."

Her eyes had strayed downward to his chest. "Hmmm?"

"The dream. Tell me what you saw."

"Oh. Something chased me through the woods. Dark storm clouds moved in and the path became cluttered with sharp stones and painful debris. Then, as whatever chased me drew closer, I looked up and saw a warrior in the distance. He had a bow notched with an arrow and was aiming at either me or whatever was behind me." She looked him in the eye. "I think the warrior was you."

"When did you have this dream? Last night?"

She shook her head. "Just before we met. At the river."

He studied her, looking for a lie. "Is that why you went with us?"

"Partly."

He drew closer. "Why did you go with us? You didn't know any of us. We could have meant you harm."

"I knew you were no threat to me."

"Because of the things you can see?"

"Yes, that's part of it."

He started to ask more questions, but snapped his mouth shut. After everything he had seen at Ituha's hut, he wasn't certain he could take anything else she told him. With a lift of his chin, he gestured in the direction they had been headed. "This way."

Soon they were standing before Dyami's tepee, both of them reluctant to enter.

Kajika lowered his voice and asked, "Do you sense anything here?"

"A little, but not like I did with Dyami."

"Good." He lifted the flap covering the entrance to the tepee then grimaced as the smell of dried blood wafted out. He reminded her, "You don't have to do this."

"I know. But if there's a chance I can help find the killer, then I'm willing."

He nodded and stepped into the tepee. Ahyoka followed close behind.

A few things had been set to right, but most of the debris remained where it had been. After what Ahyoka had said about evil clinging to Dyami's body, he found himself reluctant to touch anything.

Previously, if someone told him that he'd be standing off to the side like this, he would have laughed. But here he stood. Waiting for her to give him something he could use. Something he could hunt.

What she could see—or what she believed she could see—was beyond his understanding. The chief and Winema believed her. So, until he could prove otherwise, or unless her beliefs contradicted what he knew to be true, he would consider her advice.

Her eyes turned into that glowing amber color again.

It had startled him the first time he saw them change. He had no explanation for what made her eyes glow the way they did. It was the first piece of evidence he had to support her claim of being able to see things related to spirits. That, plus her obvious discomfort at revealing her abilities, made him rein in his doubts.

At the same time, he also had to deal with his acute awareness of her. Every time he got close to her he became uncomfortably aware of her every move. The gentle sway of her hips as she walked. How she instinctively avoided sticks and sharp rocks that might hurt her bare feet. She moved as graceful as any deer he'd ever seen cutting through the forest.

Even now, as they stood in a place covered with blood, where two killings happened just days ago, his attraction to her remained. It may be muted by his grief for his cousin and his family, but it lay there, waiting to be sparked into a flame.

To distract himself from the direction his thought had taken, he looked around the tepee. The sleeping pallet Dyami shared with Ghigau lay to his left. Just beyond was a small cradle. Above it a dream catcher swayed with the light breeze coming in from the open doorway.

The dream catcher may have kept the baby's dreams pleasant, but it hadn't kept him safe from harm.

"Are you sensing anything?" he asked to distract himself.

"Yes," she said, drawing the word out. "Some of the same dark magic I saw on Dyami is here too, but it's been trampled and scattered."

"Can you tell if it was the same person who did this?"

She looked up from her search. "I believe so. It would be very hard for two people to have the same patterns. Particularly one so heavy with malice."

"The same patterns?"

Ahyoka froze. When she finally looked up at him, he asked again, "What patterns?"

For a moment, he thought she might make a run for the door. Instead she stiffened her back. "I see things. When I want to."

"What kind of things?"

"Mother told me that people leave traces of their spirit everywhere they go. Kind of like a footprint when you walk across the soft ground."

"But you only see it when you want to?"

She nodded once, with hesitation. Her gaze darted toward the open door again.

He shifted his stance so he could sprint after her if she tried to run away. "Is that why your eyes changed color?"

She grimaced then nodded briskly and went back to her search.

He rolled the new information around. She was either a clever deceiver or there was more to this woman than he originally gave her credit for.

"It relieves me to know we may only be looking for one killer."

"True." She shuddered. "I can't imagine two people being full of such evil intent."

"Stranger things have happened," he muttered.

"If you did want to gather a few things for Dyami's burial, go ahead. This area," she gestured to the central part of the tepee, "is safe to move around in. But that area," she pointed to where Ghigau would have done their cooking, "is not. I want to take a closer look."

"Why?"

"There is an unusually dark spot there, and I want to know why."

"Show me."

She picked her way across the dirt floor, carefully avoiding certain places, then stopped. "Just there." She pointed. "Next to that knife."

If he had to guess, based on the scattered dishes and overturned chairs and personal items, the killer attacked Ghigau as she cooked. But she fought back. There was a struggle. The dark stain to the left of where they stood was most likely where she died.

He moved to get a closer look at the knife Ahyoka pointed to, but she grabbed his arm. "Let me push some of the darkness away first."

"As long as it won't take long. We need to leave soon."

Her eyes glowed again as she mumbled some kind of chant. She extended her hands in front of her and gave a few slight flicks of her wrists.

As she continued to chant softly, she raised her hands higher toward the opening in the top of the tepee. In the back of his mind, an answering chant surfaced. This one deeper and carried the sounds of a male version of hers. Instinctively he knew it had been spoken in support of her efforts.

When she finished, he noticed a difference in the air inside the tent. It felt cooler and much less oppressive. Some of his own tension and anger had melted away.

"What did you do?" he asked, awed and a little confused by

what he had just experienced.

"I asked Grandfather Wind to help me remove the killer's spiritual energies from this place. He granted my request and promised he would return them to the dark place where only the winds are free to go."

"Was that his voice I heard?"

She whipped around to face him. "You heard him?"

"I don't know who it was or what I heard, but I heard a man's voice chanting in my head."

Her mouth hinged open and she stared, unblinking.

"What's wrong? Was I not supposed to?" Great. Now he was hearing things. Next, he'd grow deer horns out of the top of his head and he'd be running around naked in the moonlight.

That might be all right if Ahyoka were with him though. Naked.

He mentally slapped himself. Now was not the time for such thoughts.

"No, I…I'm just surprised you were able to hear him. He doesn't reveal himself to many people." She tipped her head. "It's quite an honor."

"Oh." He cleared his throat. "Is it safe to get the knife now?"

"Yes. But don't touch it. The cleansing I did was quick and there may still be lingering traces."

Nodding he understood, even though he didn't really, he took a few steps then knelt in front of the knife. There was nothing unusual about it except for the spot of blood on the blade. But given what had happened, the blood wasn't unexpected.

He sensed Ahyoka's approach before he saw her.

She squatted next to him. "I was wrong. It wasn't the knife that had been covered with the bad energy." She pointed to the ground beneath the blade. "It was that."

Kajika leaned closer. He found a tuft of animal skin on the ground. It had most likely been cut off during the struggle.

But what was it from?

He reached for the bit of fur, but Ahyoka grabbed his arm. "Wait." She took a piece of linen from a nearby table and handed it to him. "Use this to pick it up so you don't have to touch it directly."

Taking the linen from her, he covered the knife, pushed it aside then picked up the bit of fur. He turned his hand over, letting the sides of the linen fall open so they could examine whatever was inside.

They both leaned closer and bumped heads.

"Owww." Ahyoka grinned as she touched her forehead. "Go ahead. You look."

He smirked, despite the seriousness of the situation, then bent to examine what was in the cloth.

"It's animal fur." He turned to allow more light onto his hand. "Wolf fur, actually."

Ahyoka frowned and looked around the tepee. "How did wolf fur get in here? Did Dyami kill one recently?"

Kajika shook his head. "Not that I know of. We don't see these kinds of wolves this far south. At least not during the warm season." He shrugged. "We might find a rogue from time to time during the coldest part of the year but never at this time. They prefer cooler areas.

"Besides, Dyami wouldn't have been hunting larger game." He continued, "Our hunting party was out. We were responsible for that. He stayed home to be with Ghigau and the baby. The only hunting he would have been doing would have been birds or rabbits. Maybe foxes. Something he could have trapped and skinned on his own."

"I need to think about this." She reached over and folded the linen around the tuft of fur then secured the ends by tying a knot. "May I keep this?"

"If you think it's important."

"It may be." She smiled and tucked the bundled linen into the pouch at her waist. "We will see."

Their eyes met. In the span of a heartbeat, he knew he couldn't take another breath without kissing her. He lowered his head slowly, giving her a chance to back away. When she didn't, he touched his lips to hers in a featherlight caress.

He fisted his hands at his sides to resist the urge to crush her body against his and consume her. The logical part of his mind that still worked warned him she might balk if she sensed the strength of his need for her.

Her lips parted on a sigh. He took advantage and tasted the edge of her lips with his tongue. She surprised him by tentatively touching her tongue to his, mimicking his movements.

Her innocent exploration rocked him to his core.

He pulled away before his control slipped. With her eyes glazed and her cheeks flushed, he wanted nothing more than to lay her down and explore every inch of her. But this was not the time. And this was certainly not the place. "We need to leave."

She blinked as if she didn't understand what he had said. Finally, she looked at her surroundings. Her spine stiffened. "Yes, we should."

He didn't think it was possible, but her face turned a deeper shade of red.

He held out his hand for hers. "Come. I will take you back to Winema so you can help her prepare the late meal."

She held his gaze for a moment, as if she wanted to say something. Finally, she nodded and put her tiny hand in his.

He breathed a sigh of relief at her easy acceptance then prayed they didn't run into any of the busybodies as they left. The older generation was far too wise in the ways of men and women to hide what had transpired between them.

There would be time to think on those things later—after Dyami's killer was found and brought to justice. Meanwhile, he needed to keep some distance between them. She was too much of a temptation and a distraction for his peace of mind.

Perhaps it would be best to ask Chief Yonaguska if one of the other warriors could escort her back to her village. That would give him a chance to pick up what they thought had been the killer's trail. Resolved that was the best course, he relaxed marginally as he led Ahyoka through the heart of the village toward Yonaguska and Winema's tepee.

And that would be that.

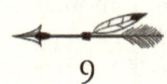

9

Ahyoka stood over the pot, stirring whatever Winema was cooking, but her mind returned again and again to the kiss she had shared with Kajika.

"How's the eagle nest soup coming along?"

"The what?" Ahyoka nearly dropped the spoon in surprise. She looked up and found Winema next to the table with her arms folded across her chest. Her look bespoke part irritation and part amusement.

"What has you so distracted?" Winema asked. "You haven't heard anything I've said since I dropped the potatoes into the pot."

"Oh, I..." Her cheeks warmed. She ducked her head, pretending interest in the bubbling soup. "I was just thinking about what we found in Dyami and Ghigau's tepee and what it may mean."

"That bit of fur? Why do you think it means anything at all?" Winema shrugged. "It could just be a scrap left from a previous hunting trip or a skin they traded for."

"Maybe." Ahyoka shrugged.

"Are you sure that's all that's on your mind?" Winema pressed.

She didn't think she could blush any more, but she did.

"That's what I thought." Winema took the spoon from Ahyoka and dropped it into the small pot on the floor near the fire. She grabbed Ahyoka's hand, pulled her to the table, and pushed her down into a chair. "Tell me what's on your mind."

"Why has Kajika not taken a wife?"

Winema's lip lifted in a half smirk. "I've never heard him give a reason. There are several maidens and even a widow or two who have made it clear they would welcome his moccasins next to their pallets."

Ahyoka blanched at the image that sprang to her mind of him taking some faceless maiden to bed. She quickly squelched the image before becoming agitated. "He hasn't given any of them reason to think he favored them over the others?"

"Not that I know of." She grunted. "And believe me, I would have heard." She leaned forward, resting her arms on the table in front of her. "Kajika is considered the most worthy warrior in our village. Any woman old enough to leave her parents would be proud to take him as husband."

"I've learned he's a well-respected hunter. I'm sure he would provide well for his family."

Winema reached across the table and placed her hand over Ahyoka's. "He's also a good man. He's kind, generous, clever, and reliable." She patted Ahyoka's hand. "And when you get to know him, you'll see he has a unique sense of humor."

"Hmmm," Ahyoka murmured.

"Why do you want to know?" Winema asked with a knowing look in her eye.

"He, uh... we... that is, I just..."

Winema chuckled. "He has you tied in knots, doesn't he?"

Heat blossomed in Ahyoka's cheeks again. "Has he ever said anything about hearing voices from the spirits?"

This time Winema laughed outright. "Kajika? Spirits?" She laughed again. "Never." When she calmed down, she added, "I would be willing to say that, even if he thought he'd received a message from an ancestor, he would find a rational explanation for it."

"Do you think he could ever accept something otherworldly?"

Winema shrugged. "Stranger things have happened." She held Ahyoka's gaze. "It would take some work to make a believer of him. Or a few events that defy everything he knows to be true."

Yonaguska's booming voice jolted them away from their conversation as he entered the tepee. "I hope that is squash soup I smell."

Just behind the chief, Kajika stepped in. "Is it a special occasion?"

"Certainly." Winema came to her feet then greeted Yonaguska with a kiss on the cheek. "We have a guest."

"So it wasn't anything I did, then?" Yonaguska teased.

"Not unless there's something you haven't told me," Winema suggested.

Their playful banter stirred something inside of Ahyoka. A deep-seated longing to be comfortable with someone as the two of them were bubbled to the surface of her heart. Even the fact that he was the chief and responsible for a large village didn't seem to matter. Obviously, theirs was a marriage based on feelings, not of responsibility.

It warmed her heart.

Her eyes skipped to Kajika and found him watching her.

That same fluttery sensation blossomed in her belly that she felt when he had kissed her. Warmth spread from her chest down to her toes and up to her ears. Strange how one man could make her feel so much with just a look.

She rose to greet him. "I'm surprised to see you. I would have thought your late meal would have been taken with the other men in the village."

He smirked. "Normally I would be." With a tip of his head in the chief's direction, he added, "Yonaguska insisted otherwise."

"I see."

"He said we needed to discuss plans for your escort back to your village."

Yonaguska slapped Kajika on the back. "That's right." He gestured to the chairs around the table. "You may as well have a seat since we're here."

"You three take your seats. I'll be right back." Winema went to the tepee opening to take a pan from the woman standing just outside. She thanked the woman then brought the pan to the table.

When Winema set the pan in the center of the table, Ahyoka saw it was full of baked cornmeal. Another woman came to the doorway. This time the pot Winema set on the table held green beans. Another quickly followed full of several ears of corn.

Ahyoka's look of surprise was addressed by Kajika. "Our people honor not only our chief but their guest." He looked to the food before them. "Apparently they are pleased by your visit."

"My visit?" Ahyoka's disbelief rang in her tone.

Chief Yonaguska laughed. "Either that or they're trying to make up for the fact that you did not plan to make a visit to our village." He leveled a look at Kajika. "But either way, the women know who aided Luyo in her time of need. And for that we are all grateful."

"We most certainly are," Winema said as she placed bowls on the table before everyone. She gestured for them to begin taking food as she took her seat.

Ahyoka tipped her head graciously. "I'm glad she and the baby are both well. I would be pleased to return for a visit next spring to see how he has grown."

"I'm sure she would be happy for you to visit." Winema winked at Yonaguska. "You never know. Maybe we'll have another grandbaby on the way by then and we can go as well."

The chief quickly changed the subject. "Speaking of traveling. What is your plan for returning Ahyoka to her home?" He looked at the food before him, but his question was obviously directed at Kajika.

"I thought I might ask Chea Sequah if he and Tuari would escort her so I could try to pick up the killer's trail again."

All three pairs of eyes landed on Kajika.

Ahyoka squelched the ache in her chest. Although she had been worried about spending more time alone with Kajika after the kiss they shared, she was also looking forward to it. She had hoped to learn more about him as they travelled. Even though she understood his need to avenge his cousin, knowing he didn't feel the same was a slap in the face.

"The hunt will have to wait," Yonaguska said flatly, brooking no argument. "You inconvenienced Ahyoka by bringing her here, with no chance to tell her family or to prepare for travel. You will make it right and escort her home. It would be insulting to do anything less." He turned his focus to his meal. "Besides, the others are needed to finish preparing the hides from your successful hunt."

Winema glanced in her direction.

Ahyoka wasn't certain, but she thought she saw Winema wink at her, yet Winema's face remained neutral.

A muscle flexed in Kajika's jaw. "You are right," he finally said. Looking to Ahyoka, he added, "It was my fault you were unable to return to your home, and I will make amends. I will have horses prepared by the first meal. We can leave as soon as you are ready."

"Very well." She couldn't help but tease him. "You said horses.

Does that mean I will be sitting on a horse of my own for the ride back?"

His eyes widened in alarm. "You can ride, can't you?"

Yonaguska chuckled. Winema covered her mouth with a rag to smother her snort of amusement.

"Yes, I was taught to ride a horse."

"Since she won't tell you, I will." Yonaguska leaned forward and rested his elbow on the table. He pointed at Ahyoka with his spoon. "This girl could probably outride every brave in our village if she wanted. Bareback or saddled." Then he pointed to Kajika with the spoon. "And that includes you."

Winema raised a brow at Kajika as if daring him to question what Yonaguska had said.

"Excellent." He looked at Ahyoka with a challenging gleam in his eye. "That means I won't be obligated to keep a snail's pace while on the trail tomorrow, then."

"Not at all." She smirked. "But it makes it rather difficult to find an already cold trail when you're flying past on horseback."

His brow furrowed in question.

"You did say you were anxious to pick up the trail you had been following?" Winema must have picked up on where Ahyoka was going with her remark. "Why can't you accomplish two things at once?"

"Your trail led you to the river, correct?" Ahyoka asked.

Kajika looked to Yonaguska, as if hoping for his intervention. However, Yonaguska was more interested in helping himself to another serving of cornbread. "It would appear so," Kajika said cautiously.

"Seems to me two eyes on a trail are better than one," Winema suggested.

"And if the trail you were following leads to or near my village, I need to know."

"If the trail leads to her village, Chief Hiamovi needs to know," Yonaguska finally spoke up. Looking at Kajika, he added, "I give you my blessing to speak to Hiamovi and his warriors freely about Dyami and Ghigau's deaths. There is no point in hiding what we know."

"Someone's life could be saved because they were prepared or alert to strangers," Ahyoka suggested. She planned to tell her chief everything, but it would be better if Kajika were there to tell his news.

Kajika nodded. "I will speak to Hiamovi either way, but I will warn him if I find the trail leads to your village."

"Thank you," Ahyoka murmured.

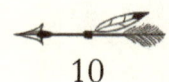

10

True to his word, Kajika had their horses packed and ready to leave before the first meal had even been served.

He'd given up on sleeping after spending a restless night alone in his tepee. Dreams of Ahyoka dancing naked in the moonlight haunted him. The stars woven into her hair beckoned to him, daring him to join her in the dance. He woke in a sweat, hard and achy with need. The thought of relieving himself held little appeal. What he needed had been several tepees away and oblivious to his discomfort.

Never had a woman plagued him so. Perhaps he would regain his sense of control once she was back in her village and there were hundreds of trees and a river between them.

If not, what then? He ruthlessly pushed the question aside as an impossibility.

He sat alone in the village gathering place. From there he saw Ahyoka leave Yonaguska and Winema's tepee. Her hair fell down her back in long silky strands instead of captured in the braids she usually wore. Images from his dream sprang to mind, making his fingers itch to feel its softness.

Instantly he was hard again. He cursed under his breath. It was going to be a long day on the back of his horse.

Unable to turn away, he watched her raise her arms in the air as if greeting the sun or the sky. Then she gathered water from the rain barrel and hurried back into the tepee. She reappeared a short time later, dressed and with her hair braided and adorned.

"Why do you never wear moccasins?" he asked when she came close enough to hear his question.

One side of Ahyoka's lip lifted in a smirk. "Good morning to you too."

"Good morning," he mumbled as he held her gaze, letting her know he expected an answer despite his rudeness.

She set her bag on the ground next to Kajika. "I prefer to be in contact with the land whenever possible. There is a lot to be learned when you're connected to the things around you. Moccasins don't block the messages, but they dampen them more than I like." She tapped her ear. "Imagine stuffing a bit of linen in your ears. You could still hear, but not as much as you normally do." Her nose crinkled. "And it makes you a little uncomfortable after a while."

A grunt was all he could offer in response. What she said made sense, but he still struggled with the idea that she picked up information from the land. The only thing he had ever learned by walking barefoot was where the stones and thorns were in his path. "You do have a pair then?"

"Of course." She sat next to him on a log. "Father has made several for me. The fur lined ones are quite nice during the colder season, but the ones he made for warmer days are almost untouched." She smiled sheepishly.

A knot loosened in his chest. If her father still made her moccasins it meant no other man had gotten close to her. The thought shouldn't please him as much as it did.

To change the subject, he asked, "Have you eaten yet?"

"I had a few berries left from the last meal, but I don't need much." She nodded to the bag she dropped next to him. "Besides, Winema packed some things for us to eat along the way."

He chuckled. "That's in addition to the bags Yonaguska is sending on the extra horse."

"What is he sending?"

Kajika shook his head. "I didn't ask. I just helped the boys ready the horses. My guess would be that Yonaguska is sending gifts to Hiamovi as well as your father."

"That isn't necessary."

He shrugged. "Not for me to decide."

She sighed.

"Are you worried about going home?"

"No. Not worried." She drew out her words.

"You don't seem excited."

"I can't explain it. I need to let my people know about the potential danger, but I dread having to explain everything to Father."

"Will he be angry with you?"

"No, but he worries. I don't think he truly understands the things I see and hear."

"What of Chief Hiamovi? Are there duties you should have been attending to?"

"Possibly. People of our village come to me when they have illnesses or injuries they do not know how to handle. But if you mean a daily activity I am responsible for, then no. Father and my brother, Maska, provide most of the village's meat from their hunts. I help wherever I can."

"Good." He checked the rise of the sun. "Have you said your farewells to Winema and Yonaguska?"

"Yes." She cast a look in the direction of Yonaguska's tepee that Kajika could only describe as longing. "We can leave whenever you are ready."

"Is that really all that you are taking with you?"

"I didn't bring anything with me but my pouch of supplies." She gave him a look of admonishment. "Which have been depleted since I have been here, so I hope you don't mind making a short stop at the river where you found me."

"As long as you don't feel the need to inspect every leaf and blossom you find there."

"Fair enough. Shall we begin then?"

Once more he wondered if her question meant more than it sounded. Despite the nagging at the back of his mind, he stood and held his hand out to help her up. "Yes. Let's be on our way."

She placed her hand in his. Her slender fingers were dwarfed in his palm. When she came to her feet, their eyes met. A ripple of awareness rushed through his body.

Startled by the sensation, Kajika stepped back to break the connection. A flash of disappointment crossed her face. Not knowing what to make of it, he waved her toward the corral. Without another word, they mounted their horses and set off for her village.

It would take almost two days to reach Ahyoka's village, but he planned to make few stops and shorten that to a day and a half. The need to search out whoever had killed Dyami and his family weighed heavily.

It pleased him to learn how comfortable with a horse she truly was. More than once she challenged him to take the more difficult path or push the horses a little more. Unfortunately, the horse carrying their supplies forced them into a slower pace.

When they stopped for water and rest, she surprised him again by helping to tend the horses.

The trail he and his trackers had followed three days earlier had faded. He found himself following the trail he and the other trackers had left instead of the killer's. When he did find the killer's trail, he was pleased they were still on the right track.

"Kajika, do you mind if we stop for a moment?"

He jerked his gaze away from the trail. "Why?"

"We passed a nice patch of pepper grass. I'd really like to gather what I can. It's hard to find at this time of the year."

Irritation rippled through him. The trail he needed to follow faded with every lift of the breeze. And she wanted to stop for grass?

"It will take no time at all," she promised. "I just need to cut them and put them in my bag. I can prepare and dry them when I get home."

"Very well," he reluctantly agreed. "It will give the horses a chance to cool off." He steered his horse toward her. "Where did you see it?"

She turned her horse around. "I'll show you." Ahyoka led them to a sunny spot in between tree clusters they had passed. She pointed to a patch of small green plants scattered across the area.

"That's what you're after?" Why was he even considering stopping for something as ordinary as grass?

"It's a wonderful plant. It adds a nice flavor to many foods and it helps with stomach ailments." She smiled. "It's rather useful."

He shrugged. "Get what you need. I'll see to the horses."

She beamed her thanks as she dismounted. After rummaging through one of the bags for a knife, she hurried off to gather her grass.

He shook his head. Why would such a small thing make her so happy? Most women were not so easy to please. If she needed a break after riding for so long, she could have just said so instead of making up a lie.

Sliding from the back of his own horse, he led the animals to a nearby shady spot. Using one of the bags of water they'd brought, he gave each of them a generous drink. Even as he worked, his eyes returned to Ahyoka.

She was a beautiful woman. The men of her village must all be blind and stupid for one of them to not take her as wife.

Unless her lack of husband had something to do with her... gifts. If she really could sense or see things no one else could, it would probably make a lot of people leery. Yonaguska said she used those gifts to help her people though. That had to count for something. Surely some man would have shown some interest in her as a woman.

Even as the thought crossed his mind, his gut churned.

Seeing her with another man, even if it was only in his head, did not sit well. It made him want to slam his fist into a tree.

Or the imaginary man's face.

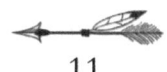

11

Her backside welcomed the relief of being off the horse. As soon as her feet touched the ground, the knots in her back began to unravel. The chattering of the birds and animals in the trees provided a sense of security. Some called out greetings. Others simply went about their day without hesitation. After all, she presented no threat to any of them.

Based on the pace he'd set, Kajika must be anxious to reach her village as soon as possible. He probably wouldn't let her stay long, but the message from the spirits urging her to stop had been so insistent she couldn't ignore it. Gathering the pepper grass had been the only excuse she could come up with.

Besides, it would be nice to replenish her supply of it. Pepper grass didn't grow anywhere near her village, so she harvested it whenever she stumbled across it. She cut several handfuls then returned to the horses.

"This should do me for a while." She held up one clump of cut greens to show Kajika her bounty.

He looked up from whatever he was doing with the horses. "Good. I just need to put the water pouch away and we can be on our way again. If you need a moment of privacy, this would be a good time to do it."

Her cheeks heated. "Good idea. Let me put these in my bag first."

She added her precious cargo to one of the satchels along with her knife then tightened the straps again. As he finished his chore, she ducked behind a cluster of trees.

"If you needed to stop for a moment, all you had to do was say something. You didn't have to lie about needing plants," he shouted to her.

She grimaced. "It wasn't a lie." Entirely.

"I'm just saying that it's all right if you can't ride as long as I am used to. I don't always think about that."

Her hand curled into a fist. She could ride as well, if not better than, most men. It irritated her to have to swallow her pride to avoid explaining the real reason for stopping. A reason that she had yet to figure out.

Why did the spirits insist they stop?

As she finished her private business, the area went unusually quiet. She righted her clothing and stepped out from behind the trees. Kajika stood ramrod straight next to the horses with his gaze fixed onto the surrounding foliage.

No birds moved or called out greetings. Even the bugs waited in silence.

"Ahyoka." Kajika's voice conveyed his unease.

"I know. I hear it too." She stepped into his line of sight and slowly moved his way. Her eyes darted from one shrub to the next as she tried to spot the threat.

The horses stepped nervously, but Kajika kept his hold on the reigns. "Come, Ahyoka."

The urgency in his voice caught her attention. She had taken only two steps in his direction when she heard rustling behind her.

She spun in time to see a black wolf leaping toward her from the shrubs. Time seemed to slow as Kajika leapt between her and the beast, his knife glinting in his hand.

"Get to the horses," he yelled.

The wolf charged him even as the words left his lips. Man and beast rolled over each other, growling and grunting with their effort to best the other. Ahyoka feared the wolf might soon overtake Kajika. The creature was larger than any wolf she'd ever seen.

She hurried to the bucking horses and tried to steady them while she reached for her satchel. One of the horses slipped out of her grasp, but she managed to hold the one that carried her things. She dug in her bag for her herbs.

"Watch out!"

At Kajika's warning, she turned. The creature had broken free of Kajika and rushed toward her. She faced the beast with her knife clutched in one hand and crushed plant leaves in the other. When the wolf sprang at her, she shouted words of protection, threw the herbs into its face, then ducked aside.

The creature let out an unholy shriek and crashed heavily to the ground. The commotion unsettled the already frightened horse. It reared back and stepped on Ahyoka as it turned to flee. Ahyoka cried out in pain, even as the smell of sweat and death clogged her senses and made her stomach turn.

The wolf shook its head and staggered to its feet. Ahyoka scrambled backward as the creature's cold, dead eyes landed upon her once again. Its lips pealed back with a snarl and the muscles along its flanks rippled in preparation to leap.

In a blur of movement, Kajika leapt at the wolf. Ahyoka caught flashes of metal as Kajika slashed at the beast. Her breath caught in her throat as she watched Kajika struggle for supremacy. She prayed frantically that he would find the strength he needed to win.

Finally, Kajika pinned the creature. His hand that clutched the knife arced downward toward his foe. At the last second, the wolf rolled aside, altering the location of Kajika's strike from its ribs to its paw. There was enough strength behind the blow that the knife cut all the way through and sank into the ground below it.

Startled birds erupted from their hiding places in the trees when the beast howled out in pain. The creature pulled itself free and scrambled away on three legs, leaving a bloody trail.

Ahyoka clutched the bottom of her leg and groaned in pain.

Kajika rushed to her side. "What's wrong?" he demanded.

"My leg." She hissed through her teeth when she tried to move her foot. "I think the horse stepped on me when she knocked me over. Something twisted badly." She rubbed the spot where the foot and leg joined.

He scanned the trees where the wolf had disappeared. "Do you think you can walk?"

She grimaced. "I'm not sure."

He adjusted his stance then picked her up into his arms. "I want to check your leg, but I'd rather do that in a safer location."

He whistled for his horse. Naturally, the well-trained beast came when called. Unfortunately, the other two did not.

Being held in his arms felt nice. Too nice. But she couldn't afford for him to see her as weak or needy. "You can put me down. I can probably stand."

He grunted and tightened his embrace. "I'm going to put you on my horse while I round up the other two. That way you'll be able to ride away if that thing comes back."

"But I can—"

"No argument. If that wolf or whatever it was comes back, you get out of here. Head to the river that's due east of us and don't look back." He leveled a hard glare at her. "Do you understand?"

"I understand you're hardheaded enough to think you can take on a grizzly bear with nothing but a stick."

"It's better than your idea of throwing grass at it." When his horse drew close, he lifted her high enough for her to grab the reins. She pulled herself the rest of the way by swinging her injured leg over. "Just do as I said. I don't want you getting in the way and getting hurt even worse," he told her. "Now promise me you'll do as I've said."

"Only if I know you'll be right behind me."

He sighed, shook his head, and muttered under his breath, "Stubborn woman."

He handed her the reigns then went to find the other two horses. Keeping one eye on the place where the wolf disappeared, she followed him toward the startled mare. It only took a few calming words to reassure the mare then Kajika climbed onto her back.

Together the two of them went in search of the supply horse. They found it hiding in a shady spot on the other side of the grove of trees. The poor thing was far more spooked and had to be calmed with soft words and strokes before it would follow them back to where they had been attacked.

"Do you think you can stand riding to the river before we stop?" he asked. "I don't believe it's far. We can look at your foot there. If it's bad, we can make camp and wait until tomorrow to ride further."

"But aren't you in a hurry to get rid of me and resume your search?"

He leveled a hard gaze at her. "I am in a hurry to resume my search, but not at your expense. We need to see about your injury."

She grimaced. "It's throbbing, but I can make it to the river."

"Good. Keep an eye on the thicker brush. Tell me if you see

that beast again."

She shuddered as she recalled the stench that had clung to the creature. She hoped they would never have to see that thing again, but something told her that was a futile wish.

12

The river bubbled as it rushed across the rocks of its bed. The birds in the trees sang to each other, and the wind danced lightly through the leaves. Peace resonated across the area and settled within Ahyoka like a balm to a wound after battle.

Kajika sat on the patch of soft grass next to Ahyoka. "How is your foot?"

She rubbed the place that hurt the most. "Painful."

"Do you think you can ride?"

She grimaced. "I could if I had to, but if I were advising someone else on tending this injury, I'd tell them to rest with the foot propped up on something."

His jaw tensed then he sighed. "I'll settle the horses and have a look around. I want to make sure that wolf didn't linger."

"You can leave me here if you need to return to your village. I can find my way home tomorrow. I'm sure Father could bring the horse back to you once he returns from his hunt."

Kajika's frown deepened. "I will see you safely to your father's tepee."

"But—"

"What do you need from the supplies?"

Seeing there would be no arguing with him—not that she really wanted to anyway—Ahyoka told him, "A blanket to lie on and a small cup for mixing herbs."

"That's all?"

She nodded to the river. "There's water within crawling

64

distance. As long as I still have a few pieces of dried meat and some berries in my bag, I'll be fine for the night."

"I'll find something more for us to eat than that."

Ahyoka suppressed her grin. Of course he would. He wouldn't be able to help himself. Warriors were providers and protectors. Their pride would not allow them to do less. Even though she could take care of herself, it would be nice to let her guard down and focus on healing.

She touched his arm. "Thank you."

For a moment, his fierce expression softened. "You're welcome."

The whinny of one of the horses broke their connection. With a quick scan of the area, Kajika returned once again to his protector role. "There was something odd about the wolf that attacked us," he finally commented. "It smelled as if it had rolled across something dead."

"It wasn't a wolf," she confessed. "At least, not anymore. I believe what attacked us was a skinwalker."

"A what?"

"A skinwalker. Someone who can take the shape or form of an animal."

He stared behind them, in the direction they'd come. Then he sat down heavily next to her. "That's what you were telling me about yesterday."

"Yes. The reason it smelled like it had rolled over something dead is because part of it is dead."

His frown turned into a scowl.

"Many medicine men are gifted with the ability to commune with animals," she explained. "Some become so in tune with their animal spirit guides that they can transform into whatever animal they are closest with. Skinwalkers are men who are not naturally gifted with that ability but may take on the appearance of an animal by wearing its pelt. Mother believed one had to dip into dark magic to override nature like that. If that is what we're dealing with, there is no telling what they're capable of doing."

"You really believe this is some kind of dark magic?"

"I have seen enough signs to believe it's possible."

Kajika's jaw flexed as he fell silent. After a few moments, he asked, "What were the leaves you threw at it when it charged at you? They sure made that thing mad."

"It was an ordinary mix of herbs." She played with a piece of grass next to her and avoided looking at him, but she felt the weight of his stare.

"Just herbs?"

"It wasn't the herbs that burned but rather the power of the words behind it."

"Explain."

She took a deep breath. Every time he asked her for an explanation, she felt as if she were giving him reason to push her away. But she wasn't going to lie to him. "I asked the Corn Mother for her protection and she gave it. What I threw were ordinary herbs, some I carry with me everywhere I go, but I left it up to the Corn Mother to do with them as she judged best."

Once again he fell silent. Part of her wished she could read his thoughts. Then again, she might not like what she would find if she could.

"Do you think that skinwalker killed Dyami?" he finally asked.

"It's possible."

"Why?"

"That I do not know."

The muscle in his cheek flexed. "I need to see to the horses." He rose to his feet.

Her heart flipped in her chest as she looked up at him. The sun fell across his shoulder and chest creating shadows in the recesses of his muscular form. He was a handsome man. Despite her inexperience, her body knew what it wanted and, at this moment, it wanted him.

Even the pain in her foot didn't dampen her stirrings of longing.

"I'll bring your things in a moment."

"Thank you," she murmured.

With practiced ease, he removed the supplies and blankets from each of the horses then led them to the river. She couldn't hear what he said, but his lips moved as he spoke to them. Even as he tended to the animals, he kept one eye on the surrounding land.

She prayed whatever had attacked them would stay away. At least for the night.

Rest easy Spirit Talker.

Danger is gone.

We watch.

We warn.

"Thank you," she whispered to the spirits.

Not wanting to interrupt him, she scooted to the river's edge and dipped her feet into the water. She sighed as the cool water swirled over her injury. A refreshing dip would be nice, but the strain on her foot probably wouldn't be worth it. Instead she scooped water in her hands and rinsed the dust and sweat away from her face and arms.

She remained where she sat even after Kajika had finished watering the horses.

"I would have carried you. All you had to do was ask," he said as he took a seat next to her.

"I didn't want to disturb you while you were tending the horses. Besides, it wasn't far."

He grunted in response then handed her a drinking pouch. "I think we're safe for now," he declared, then took a long drink from his own pouch.

"We are."

He looked at her as if waiting for an explanation or more information.

"They told me the danger was gone and they would warn me if it returned."

"Who is they?"

Her heart warmed to see no veiled humor or criticism in his expression. Only curiosity. "I'm not always certain which voices I hear. I believe the words come from the animals in the area or the spirits that inhabit the land and water. Most of the time it sounds like a blending of many. Sometimes I even hear our ancestors."

"Like the fox you spoke to the other night?"

"Yes. But he was only one voice. He came specifically to speak with me because of what had happened in your village." When he didn't laugh at her, she added, "I sensed he may be an ancestor who stays to protect his home. Maybe a former chief or medicine man. Someone quite old and wise with strong ties to that area."

"Does that mean I should be careful when hunting foxes near the village?"

She smiled. "He probably knows how to stay out of your sights. But it wouldn't hurt to listen closely to your gut if you do find one. It will tell you if you shouldn't make the kill."

"I'll try to remember that." He looked down at her foot. "How does it feel?"

"The cool water helps, but it is throbbing a bit. I think I have everything I need to make a paste of herbs that will ease it."

"Good."

She gestured to the flowing water. "If you wish to rinse off in the river, go ahead."

"Is that a nice way of telling me I smell like the horses?"

A laugh bubbled up. "No. I thought the water looked refreshing and that you might enjoy it while we had a moment."

"It does." He slipped the bag he carried across his chest over his head and dropped it on the ground. He also pulled the knife from the sheath strapped to his leg and lay it next to her. "I believe I will take your advice."

"I didn't mean—"

He winked then waded in.

Even at its deepest, the water only reached the top of his knees. She watched in fascination as he knelt and used his hands to scoop water up to his face. Her mouth went dry watching the drops roll down his arms and chest. The urge to follow those droplets burned within her belly.

She had never been near a man who fascinated her so. Even before she had given up her girlish fantasies of being wanted by one of her people's braves, she didn't recall ever feeling this way.

The likelihood of her ever taking a husband was small. At her age, the girls of her village had been wives for several seasons and most had given birth to at least one child. Why should she miss the opportunity to learn what went on between a man and a woman?

Kajika had given her more than one look that made her think he'd considered her as a woman. But her place as his chief's honored guest almost ensured he would treat her as family.

Unless she somehow changed his mind.

But what could she do? Other than what she had observed in her dealings within her village, she knew little of what went on between men and women. She knew what could ultimately happen, but not how to bring it about.

Honorable warrior.

Be honest, Spirit Talker.

Her thoughts were interrupted when Kajika waded back to where she sat. The sunlight reflected off the drops of water that he hadn't shaken off and made her fingers itch with the need to touch.

"Is that better?" he asked when he reached her.

She swallowed, trying to get moisture back into her mouth. "Much."

Their gazes met and she had the sensation of the world dipping to one side. How did one man affect her so?

"I, uh…" He gestured to the water. "I saw several fish. I thought I could build a small fire so we could cook whatever I caught for our meal."

"That would be nice. How can I help?"

"You need to stay off your foot. But you can watch the fish while it cooks."

She smiled at his thoughtfulness. "All right."

"I'll gather wood for the fire. We will stay here for the night." He fetched her knife from her satchel.

"Keep this close. It's not big, but it's better than nothing." He glanced about the area. "I won't go far, but I don't want to leave you here unprotected."

His reliance on his weapons amused her. "I am never unprotected."

He frowned. "You were hurt."

"Not mortally."

He grunted then stomped away.

She smiled. Whatever had attacked them had left the area. If it had remained, the spirits would alert her. She had confidence in that knowledge, but he did not.

It was unfortunate that she couldn't show him what she could see and hear. Maybe then he'd understand. Of course, if she had that ability, she would have shown her father and everyone in their village by now. Maybe then they wouldn't think her strange.

13

After building the small fire, he waded back into the river. He'd been able to catch two fish easily, but he wanted to catch a couple more.

His need to demonstrate his ability to provide food for Ahyoka bothered him. Providing for his village came easily. He'd always had successful hunts. He had even helped provide for his mother and father until they went to live near his brother. But never for one special person.

He kept one eye on her as she tended the cooking of the fish. She had insisted on adding some of her grasses and herbs. She seemed to know what they could be used for. Hopefully that meant she knew which tasted best too. He dreaded the possibility of choking down bad food to avoid hurting her feelings.

"This one is just about done," she called out from the river bank.

He speared another fish then held it up for her to see. "Good. I have another to go on the fire in its place."

By the time they finished catching, cooking, and eating their meal, the sun had tipped behind the line of trees. He had been pleasantly surprised by how flavorful the fish had been. They were probably the best he'd ever eaten. He'd even enjoyed sharing stories while they ate.

Even now, with her injured foot, she insisted on taking their bowls and things to the river to wash. While she did that, he dug out a blanket for her to use for the night.

After she'd repacked their things, they settled near the fire.

"Do you need anything else to be able to make your salve for your foot?"

"No. I went ahead and used the things I had with me and made it while the fish cooked."

"Oh. It must not have been too complicated to do then. I didn't see you working on it."

"Not really. It's a simple mixture." She lifted her foot where he could see it. "I put some on already. The part that hurt is much better."

"Good."

She pulled a small pouch out of her bag. "Did you injure anything during the struggle?"

"No. Nothing."

"You can't tell me that you didn't strain or fall on something." She wiggled the pouch. "I'd love to show you how well this works. It's something I made up on my own."

He sighed. "All right. There's a place on my back you can try it on."

Her smile almost lit up the night sky.

He scooted closer and turned so she could reach his back. When she opened the pouch, a strong smell of herbs floated around to him. The first touch of her hand against his skin sent jolts of awareness shooting through him. Was it her or the mixture coating her palm?

Despite their smaller size, her hands were confident in their movement. She managed to find exactly where the ache lay and worked that area until it loosened. When she moved up to the place where his arm met his body, he couldn't hold in the sigh of contentment. The circling motion of her hands only relaxed him further.

She surprised him by shifting until she faced him and working on his front.

In her new position, he could watch the flickering light of the fire on her face. Occasionally she bit her lip, but he doubted she even realized it. Every drop of her attention remained on him and what she was doing to him.

The strain of being on a horse all day as well as the fight with the wolf-thing melted away. If there were any magic to be found, it might just be in her fingers.

Before she reached his hand, he leaned forward and kissed her.

She froze for a moment, but when she responded, it felt as if he'd stepped into a blazing fire. Her hands slid up to his neck and she leaned into him. The softness of her body warmed him and made him want things he shouldn't have. Still he deepened their kiss, urging her to open to him. When she did, he teased her tongue with his own, coaxing her further. Her innocence mixed with her enthusiasm made an intoxicating combination.

With no thought of how far it might go, he pulled her into his lap. She wiggled and squirmed, pressing against his erection, inflaming him further. He finally broke free of their kiss and buried his face in her neck. He inhaled deeply, drinking in her scent even as he struggled to gain control.

Her hands fluttered across his back, leaving trails of warmth where she touched.

He ran his tongue up the side of her neck until he found the base of her ear. He whispered, "We should stop," even as he nuzzled that spot.

"Why?" Her voice came out in a husky whisper.

"Because…" He skimmed his hand down her back and pulled her closer to his hardened cock, hoping for a moment of relief. "Because my chief ordered me to protect you."

She leaned back and looked him in the eye. "You aren't doing anything I don't like or don't want."

"I don't wish to dishonor you or betray my chief's trust."

"You could only do that if I told you to stop and you didn't."

He considered her words and the sincerity in her eyes. He nodded then captured her lips once more.

And once again the heat of their coupling engulfed them. He rolled to the side, pinning her beneath him. He ran one hand down her side, memorizing her curves. The urge to rip away the offending fabric between them rode him hard.

Her leg rose up to his hip, pushing her dress upward, exposing her core to him. Uncertain about her experience, he didn't want to push her. He rolled onto his back, taking her with him. She leaned away and gave him a look of uncertainty. "Sit astride," he whispered, "like you would a horse."

Once she was settled, she instantly relaxed again. Her gaze danced across his bare chest and her hand quickly followed. He startled when her nail raked across his nipple, making her eyes widen. Then she gave him a wicked grin and leaned over, making her hair fall forward. She pressed timid kisses to his chest. They were light, almost innocent points of contact, but they sent jolts of awareness through his body.

Using his grip on her waist, he ground his budging crotch against her center to show how she affected him. She made a sound much like the purr of a cat. He wanted nothing more than to rip his breeches away and drive upward into her body, but his gut warned he needed to go slower with her.

He slid his hand up her back and found the back of her neck. He urged her to slide up and kiss him again. Something about her lips drove him wild. She gave in, but only for a moment.

When she sat up, she reached for the laces of her dress at her back then pulled the material up and over her head. He lay in stunned silence, drinking in the sight.

"Beautiful," he murmured as he reached to touch her. He ran the topside of his fingers over one of her breasts then the other. When he looked up, he found she had closed her eyes, as if she were absorbing every touch.

He hooked his hand behind her neck again and pulled her down for another kiss. Her bare chest met his and sent another wave of heat crashing through him.

He let up on their kiss and urged her forward. "Scoot up," he told her.

She blinked, not comprehending what he wanted. He scooted down and showed her where he wanted her. Her eyes widened when his mouth came to rest at the juncture of her legs. From his vantage point, he could see all the way up the front of her body.

He encouraged her to spread her knees and lower herself closer to his face. He didn't think it possible for her to widen her eyes any further, but she did when he ran his tongue along her center. She gasped when he found the place at the top of her folds that could bring her pleasure.

It only took a slight adjustment to gain better access to her opening and slip his finger inside. When he pumped that finger in and out of her channel in time with his licks on her swollen bud, she moaned and rocked against his finger.

She was ripe with desire and he wanted nothing more than to bury himself inside of her. But he wanted to see her find her pleasure first. He kept up a steady rhythm with his finger and tongue, using his teeth only to add a slightly different sensation from time to time. Her legs began to shake, warning him she was close. One last suckle on the tiny bud had her shouting out her relief.

He drank in her juices as if it had come from the finest berries in the land. She slumped forward, but he encouraged her to scoot down his chest. Her heart hammered against her chest and she sucked in huge gulps of air.

As she tried to resettle against his chest, he loosened the ties of his pants and pushed them down, freeing his aching cock. He slid her further down his chest until their hips were aligned. Then he rubbed his cock against her opening, coating it until it slid freely through her folds. He rocked back and forth until she lifted her head and sought out his lips.

It took all of his willpower to keep his kiss from consuming her. She touched her tongue to his then a battle for control ensued. Their hands explored every part they could reach. Sweat coated the space between them, and their breaths came in pants and gasps. Finally, he could take no more.

He reached between them and guided his cock to her opening. She paused just as he entered her channel, but then allowed her weight to drop. She let out a gasp and froze as soon he was seated all the way inside of her. The warmth of her channel was bliss. But even through his haze he sensed something was different about their joining. He gritted his teeth and allowed her a moment to adjust to him and the sensation.

As soon as she tried to move, he tightened his grip on her waist and guided her into a rhythm that suited them both. She quickly adapted, and before long, he felt a fluttering around his cock. "Kajika, it's... I'm..."

"Let go. I'm right here." He reached down and found her swollen bud. It only took a flick or two until she surrendered. With one last thrust, he joined her.

She slumped against his chest, boneless.

As his ability to think came back to him, he realized what she had done. "That was your first time to be with a man, wasn't it?"

She stiffened then slowly pulled up until she looked him in the eye. "How did you know?"

He shrugged. "Mostly a guess. But there were a few signs."

She started to move away, but he stopped her. "Why?"

"Why what?"

"Why didn't you tell me? Why me?"

She tried to pull away again, but he kept his hold on her.

"I—" She bit her lip. "You may find this hard to understand, but I wanted to know what it was like between a woman and a man."

"But why me?"

"Because you…" She looked away. "You don't look at me as if I'm something to be afraid of or something you don't understand. A couple of times you looked at me as something you actually wanted. And I wanted you also. I thought, if it were something we both felt, then maybe it would be good. Maybe it would be okay to learn about things that I will never get another chance to learn."

His mouth nearly fell open from his surprise. "What do you mean you'll never get another chance to learn?"

She rolled off and lay beside him, and since she didn't try to move any further away, he let her.

"I mean that I've realized I will never have a husband to show me the things that go on between a man and woman."

"Why not?"

The look she gave him held years of pain from rejection. "Because no one wants a wife who can hear voices that no one else hears and knows things that no one else knows." She shrugged. "It frightens them."

"So you weren't just hoping to improve your position by taking a warrior to husband?"

She wrinkled her nose at him. "No. My father is an honored warrior and so is my brother. Our people may be uncomfortable with me, but they honor and respect them. Unless the Great Spirit chooses to take them both before me, I will be provided for until I die. I have no need of a husband." Her eyes widened in alarm. "Did you think I meant to entice you to take me to wife?"

He shrugged. "It wouldn't be the first time someone tried that."

She placed her hand on his arm. "Kajika, please understand that I expect nothing from you after we find the killer. I'll return to my village and you are free to return to yours, and then you never have to speak to me again."

He frowned at her.

"I would hope that you wouldn't be so cold," she said, rolling free. "But I don't expect you to take me to wife."

"What if there is a child?"

"Then I will raise him or her and love them with everything I have."

He fell silent as he struggled to decide how he felt about her revelation. Part of him felt relieved that she had no expectation of turning his world upside down with demands of marriage. But oddly, part of him was disappointed she didn't want more.

Instead of scaring him, the thought of her bearing his child sent a ripple of longing through his chest.

14

Welcome, Spirit Talker.
  Much to tell.
  Welcome.

Ahyoka rode into her village next to Kajika just before sunset. The people of her village who were milling about stopped and stared. It felt strange to have her arrival be noticed. Usually she slipped in and out without raising any interest among her tribe members.

The wary looks from the people of her village were nothing new. It had to be Kajika's presence that brought the elders out in droves. By the time they reached the far side of the village, Chief Hiamovi had been alerted and stood ready to greet them. She whispered a prayer that he was more welcoming to Kajika than he normally was with her—even if their tribes didn't get along at all times.

Kajika dismounted then came to help her from the saddle. She smiled in gratitude at his thoughtfulness.

Hiamovi tried to mask the frown that creased his brow as he greeted them.

"Ahyoka, we began to think you had floated down the river that you love so much."

"My apologies, Chief Hiamovi," Ahyoka said. "My day was unexpectedly interrupted and I had no opportunity to send word." She shifted her weight to her uninjured foot and gestured to Kajika. "Chief Hiamovi, this is Kajika," Ahyoka told him. "He is

Chief Yonaguska's most honored warrior."

"Chief Yonaguska sends his regards," Kajika said. "He also apologizes for detaining Ahyoka. His wife, Winema, very much appreciates being granted an opportunity to visit with her. You also have my apologies for requesting Ahyoka come to my village without first alerting you."

Hiamovi grunted. "Yonaguska. I haven't heard his name mentioned in many seasons." He crossed his arms. "His village is well beyond the river. How did you make your way that far without a horse?"

"As I said, that was my fault." Kajika glanced toward the group who had crowded nearby. "But perhaps that explanation would be better left for later."

"Very well." Hiamovi said to Ahyoka, "Your father will be happy to know you are returned unharmed."

Ahyoka cringed. "He returned early from their hunt?"

"Not yet. I sent word for him just this morning that you had been gone for more than two moons without word."

She nodded her understanding. It was good to know that, if she were ever in a spot, someone would come looking for her in a short amount of time. Unfortunately, her father would worry until he saw her again.

"I expect he'll return soon," Hiamovi told her.

"I would be happy to explain what happened to him as well," Kajika said.

Hiamovi chuckled. "You may as well plan on it." He gestured to the seating area next to his tepee. "Meanwhile, come. I'm sure you are weary from your journey and in need of refreshment." He summoned one of the women who hovered nearby and instructed her to bring water, fruit, and bread.

The area Hiamovi pointed them toward consisted of two logs covered by blankets and two sturdy chairs. A couple of blankets lay on the ground near one of the logs.

Kajika took Ahyoka's arm and steered her to one of the chairs, forcing her to protest under her breath. He finally relented and assisted her onto one of the blankets. While she appreciated his help, it drew unnecessary attention her way. Things went much easier when she simply remained in the background.

Hiamovi lumbered over to the chair he traditionally used and sat down.

Kajika sat on the log closest to Ahyoka instead of next to the chief, making more than one set of eyebrows raise in question. Oddly, Kajika didn't seem concerned with the looks they received.

"So tell me how Ahyoka came to be in Chief Yonaguska's care," Hiamovi prompted.

Leaning forward with his elbows resting on his knees, Kajika explained. "One of our hunters and his family were killed several moons ago. I followed the trail of someone we thought might be involved. That trail led me to the river west of your village."

The chief looked at Ahyoka. "The one that you frequent?"

She nodded.

"When I found Ahyoka at the river, I questioned her." He glanced at her. "Her answers and her claim to know Chief Yonaguska and his wife made me think it would be best to take her to our village for further questioning." He shrugged. "Of course, once Chief Yonaguska and his wife saw her, she was welcomed as an honored guest."

"Winema was a gracious host. She insisted I stay with them," Ahyoka added.

A murmur went through the elders who hovered nearby.

"What of this killing? You believe the person responsible left your village and traveled this way?" Hiamovi asked.

"The trail we originally followed led us this direction," Kajika explained. "However, since we didn't find anyone when we searched, we can only guess that we were following the killer. We don't know that for certain."

"Do you have any reason to believe this person may kill again?"

"Possibly." Kajika glanced at the handful of people gathered near Hiamovi. He was obviously uncomfortable speaking of such matters in front of so many people. "We believe the husband was killed while hunting in the nearby woods, but the wife and child later that evening."

The women hovering nearby let out a collective gasp.

"A child's life was taken?" one of the elders asked.

"Yes," Kajika answered.

Hiamovi exchanged a look with one of the elders.

"Has anyone spotted strangers wandering nearby in the last two days?" Kajika asked, taking control of the conversation.

"No, but most of our hunters are still in the hunting grounds."

"Has anyone from your village gone missing?" Kajika asked.

Hiamovi raised one brow. "Other than Ahyoka?"

"Yes," Kajika replied.

Hiamovi looked to the group of elders. They each shook their heads. "No," Hiamovi answered for them.

"Is anyone acting strange or out of character?" Ahyoka interjected.

After his initial surprise at her question, Hiamovi looked once more to the group of elders. Again, they shook their heads. "No."

There was a pause and then Hiamovi held up one finger. "Although." He paused. "There was a disturbance last night. At least we think it happened last night."

"You sound unsure," Kajika pointed out.

"A tepee was ransacked. It wasn't discovered until this morning, so we aren't certain when it occurred."

"Was anything taken?" Kajika asked.

"We believe a wild animal did it, so it is possible food was taken. But we won't know until the owner searches their things."

Kajika and Ahyoka exchanged a quick glance.

"A wild animal?" Kajika asked.

Ahyoka asked at the same time, "Who does the tepee belong to?"

Hiamovi tipped his head to Ahyoka. "Your father."

Ahyoka sat up straight. "Father's tepee?" She struggled to gain her feet.

Kajika stood then reached to help her.

"I should see if anything is damaged," she explained.

"I'll go with you," Kajika said.

She lowered her voice. "You need to finish explaining to Chief Hiamovi what is going on." She glanced to where the chief sat watching their exchange. "I can find you after I've looked over our things."

She tried to step around him, but he grabbed her hand. "I don't think you should go alone."

"It will be fine." She tried to smile. "You forget I'm not completely helpless."

"Perhaps not, but you are injured, and if a wild animal was responsible, it could have gotten back in." He leveled a look on her that said it was pointless to argue. "I'm going with you."

"But it would be considered disrespectful," she whispered then cut her eyes to the chief to convey her meaning.

"I'm sure Chief Hiamovi understands my position." Kajika didn't bother to lower his voice. He looked at Hiamovi but continued to speak to her. "My chief placed you in my care and charged me with your protection. Until I can return you into your father's care, I will do exactly that."

"Use what is left of the daylight to go look over your father's things. When you are finished, return and tell us what you have found. I will have a meal prepared to honor our guest." He waved them on. "You may finish your tale as we eat."

Ahyoka quickly looked down to hide her surprise at the chief's willingness to send Kajika with her. He was normally rigid with his formality, particularly with anyone he felt held some rank. She shook off her questions as Kajika offered his arm for her to grasp as she limped around the log.

"We will return shortly," she assured Hiamovi. "I just need to see what damage has been done."

Hiamovi had already leaned over to speak to the elder sitting next to him, so she had no way of knowing whether he'd heard her. Not that is mattered if he did. Rarely did any of the village elders pay attention when she spoke that's why she didn't bother most of the time.

She shook her head and let Kajika lead her away.

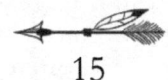

15

Leaning heavily on Kajika's arm, Ahyoka hobbled as fast as she could.

"We're in no rush," he told her quietly.

"You may not be, but the sun is fading fast. I need to know if our tepee needs repairs."

"Very well," he scooped her up in his arms as if she weighed nothing. "Which way?"

Ahyoka's breath caught in her chest. The slow burn she felt whenever she was near him burst into flame. The solid feel of his chest next to hers and his arms cradling her sent her into sensory overload. Her mind lost the ability to form any kind of response. She resorted to pointing in the right direction.

Once again, the sight of his lips at such close range distracted her. Now that she had sampled them, she craved them even more.

"Tell me when we get to yours," he reminded her.

She blinked and pulled her eyes away from his face and looked at their surroundings. "Over there," she directed him around the small garden patch. "That one," she pointed to a large tepee clearly set apart from the main part of the village near the cluster of trees.

Kajika frowned. "Why is it set away from the main part of the village?"

She shrugged one shoulder. "It's more comfortable for everyone if we stay out here."

His frown deepened, but he said nothing.

As he neared her tepee, she sensed things were off about the area. Without a second thought, she opened herself up to the elements.

Spirit Talker.
Anger and vehemence passed this way.
It tainted our home.
Beware. Beware.

Kajika tensed then suddenly came to a halt. "What did you just do?"

"Nothing, I—" Looking down, she realized her feet were not touching the ground. The messages and energies she normally drew on would have traveled through Kajika's body to reach her.

"I'm sorry." She wiggled and tried to get down, but he held tight. "I forgot I wasn't in direct contact with the land."

"It felt as if I had stepped into a warm stream of water." He looked at her. "Is that what it's like for you every time you do that thing with your eyes?"

Her cheeks heated. Now he was really going to think she was some kind of freak of nature. "It was the land's energies trying to reach me." She squirmed again. "If you'll put me down, you won't have to worry about it."

He hesitated, as if debating what to do, then he slowly lowered her until her feet touched the ground.

Putting her weight on her uninjured foot, she steadied herself then gave him a tight smile. "Thank you."

"Will that...?" He gestured to the ground near her feet. "That won't make your injury worse, will it?"

"No. Actually, it will speed the healing."

"Interesting," he murmured.

She wasn't sure if he were contemplating jumping on his horse and riding away as fast as he could or if waiting for her to grow another head.

"This area," she pointed to the clearing where their tepee stood, "has a lot of natural energy. It's one of the reasons we chose to live here." She looked toward the village. "Most people sense it, but don't know what it is. I think it disturbs them, so they shy away from it." She shrugged. "My brother and I thrive on it. We absorb it, sift the messages the land give us, and use it to help others. To help our village."

"What is it telling you?"

"That something foul has been here. Something seeking

vengeance and power."

"And it was looking for something in your father's tepee?"

She looked at the structure of sticks and skins. Somehow the designs, so lovingly painted by her own hand, now seemed tainted. "Apparently."

"Stay here." He pulled his knife from its sheath and moved silently to the tepee entrance. With slow movements, he pulled the flap aside and peered inside. His head turned one way, then the other, as he scanned the interior.

He shot her a look that promised retribution if she didn't stay where she was then he disappeared into the darkened structure.

Ahyoka held her breath and waited for him to reappear. She didn't need him to tell her there was nothing inside. The land whispered to her. It begged for a cleansing to be rid of the evil that had darkened the purity of their home. She yearned to light the fire and banish the shadows that lingered.

He finally stepped out. "It's safe."

She limped to the entrance. "Safe is relative," she told him as she secured the flap to the outside. She prayed the fresh air and light would dissipate enough of the ill feelings that they wouldn't linger and require a deep cleansing.

She ducked her head and stepped inside.

The scene looked much like what they had found in Dyami and Ghigau's tepee. Chairs were toppled. Herbs and dried roots were scattered. Pots and pans tossed.

Finding her sleeping mat and blanket shredded disturbed her more than she expected. It looked as if a wild animal had used its sharp claws to destroy it.

She looked at Kajika. His lips were set in a firm line.

"What do you see?" he asked.

"It looks much the same as Dyami's. The lingering spirit traces are similar." She scanned the room until a particularly dark spot near her mother's chest caught her attention.

She hobbled over to take a closer look.

There on the ground next to the chest were the remains of a rabbit. Around the rabbit's chest, just above the point that it had been sliced open, lay one of her mother's bracelets.

Tears clouded her eyes and instinctively she reached for the bracelet, but Kajika grabbed her hand and stopped her. "Are you sure you want to touch that?" He tipped his head toward the rabbit. "More than once you've told me not to touch things the killer has handled. Wouldn't this be the same?"

She looked down at the bracelet. "Yes." She stood, forcing him to his feet as well. Sniffing back her tears, she admitted, "You are right. Thank you."

"This is something that is important to you?" He pointed to the bracelet.

"It was my mother's."

"Ah." He nodded. "Let me get it."

"You shouldn't touch it either."

"I know. Do you have something I can wrap it in?"

She grabbed the first linens she found and an old scrap of hide. "Here. You can use these."

"Why don't you finish looking around to make sure there aren't any other surprises like this?"

"That's probably a good idea."

She scanned the room again, much more carefully this time. However, her attention continued to be drawn to where Kajika worked to clean up the rabbit and the bracelet.

Why would someone do that? Not only to the rabbit, but also to the bracelet? Now that she had stepped away, she realized there may have been some ritual involved. The purpose of it she couldn't say. She had never been taught that kind of thing.

Seeing nothing else that could harm them, she limped closer to find out if he had finished. His gaze lingered on the drawing of the wall not far from him. To answer his unspoken question, she told him, "That is my brother's work. He is able to put anything he sees onto parchment or skins."

"I'm impressed." He studied the image a moment more then looked her way. "I'm guessing you didn't find anything else that concerned you?"

"No."

He nodded. "Good." He reached for her hand and helped her around a small pile of debris.

She winced when she stepped on something that turned her foot in an odd direction. After all of the jostling she'd endured through the day, her ankle had begun to throb.

"Come." He helped her through the entry way. "You need to get off that foot and rest."

"I'm all right," she weakly protested.

"You're tired. I'll take you back so your chief can prove to me that he is capable of taking care of his people even though he couldn't be bothered to secure your dwellings while you were away."

For the second time in a day, she was rendered speechless. Other than her brother or father, no one had ever expressed any concern over her treatment. And to question her chief's behavior toward her was unheard of.

What did it mean?

16

Kajika's irritation with Ahyoka's chief and the people of her village grew as the evening wore on. More than once he had to stop Ahyoka from getting up to refill her drink. For some reason, the women who brought the food avoided her.

He didn't understand it and was offended for her.

When the chief called for another round of sweet cakes, Kajika declined. "Ahyoka needs to rest and tend her injury, and I need to prepare a place for us to sleep."

"Prepare a place? Why can she not simply return to her own tepee?"

The look Kajika turned on the unaware, oversized peacock was enough to silence those sitting next to him, but obviously not enough to impact the chief.

"A few scattered linens shouldn't bother her," the chief said.

"No, but the blood and smell from the slaughtered animal we found will take some time to clean. Especially after sitting in the stale heat for more than one turn of the sun."

"Animal? What animal?" the chief blustered. "No one told me there was a dead animal in there. You must be mistaken."

Keeping a tight leash on his temper, Kajika slowly came to his feet. He retrieved the carcass from where he had stashed it next to the pile of stacked wood. After he loosened the knot on the linens he'd wrapped it in, he dropped the bundle at the chief's feet. "I'm quite certain."

Ignoring the looks of outrage and whispered murmurings, he

went to Ahyoka and held out his hand to help her up. This time there was no question in her eyes, only a smile. She placed her tiny fingers on his palm and came to her feet.

"I know of a comfortable spot we can use for the night," she told him.

He allowed her to hobble out of the chief's sitting area before sweeping her into his arms. "Tell me which way to go."

"What about your things?"

"I will get them once you've shown me this comfortable spot and I am satisfied it is safe."

She directed him to a cluster of trees closer to the nearby stream. Without the light of day, he couldn't see it, but he felt the cooler air and heard the bugs that made their home in the water.

"My mother told me when I was a little girl that this was a special place. She said if I was ever alone and afraid I should come here and I would be protected."

"By whom?"

"The spirits who guard the river, the land, and the wind. She said they often meet here to exchange stories of their adventures. Their combined powers would watch over me until either she or my father came for me."

He stopped at the edge of a half-circle of trees and set her on her feet. Before he released her, he asked, "Did you believe her?"

"I did." She shrugged. "I still do."

Her talk of spirits and energies of the land were things he had trouble believing in. But the tiny woman in his arms had made him challenge a great many things he had believed to be true over the past few days.

The place she led him to was a naturally defensible spot. Trees offered a barrier. Nearby animals and bugs would warn them if anyone approached.

If she felt safe here, then who was he to question her reasons?

"Find us a spot for the bedroll. I'll return with our supplies. Is there anything else you need?"

"A bath would be nice," she said hopefully.

An image of her coming out of the pond near his village sprang to mind, forcing him to clamp down on his reaction. "If the river is as close as I think it is, we can arrange that." He took two steps away then stopped and turned back to her. With a stern look, he told her, "Wait for me. We'll bathe together."

Without giving her a chance to argue, he resumed his trek to the corral to retrieve their supplies. As soon as he was sure he was out of her view, he quickened his pace. He didn't trust her to do as she was told, and he was not missing his chance to see her up close in nothing but water drops and moonlight.

17

Ahyoka remained in awe of Kajika's ability to walk without making a sound. Even the animals and insects allowed him to pass without notice. As he made his way back to the main part of the village, she soaked in the view.

He was a handsome man. And a powerful warrior. Any woman would be proud to claim him. Was she wrong to hope for a chance to win his favor?

Destiny.

She lifted her gaze to the treetops and listened to the spirits. Their voices comforted her fears and reminded her of her heritage. Most people didn't understand her gifts—some even feared them—but that didn't mean she was lacking. Surely she had something to offer a husband.

The crunch of a snapped branch drew her attention. She pulled her knife from her pocket and opened her senses.

The young watcher.

He comes.

The watcher. The spirits probably meant one of Wahkan's sons. They often stood watch on the edges of the village. Their warnings of approaching strangers had served the village more than once.

She didn't have to wait long to see Quanah, Wahkan's youngest son, peeking around a tree not far from where she stood.

"Good evening, Quanah."

Her greeting had the intended effect. The boy stepped out and glanced about the clearing.

"Do you come alone?" she asked.

He nodded.

She gestured him forward. "Did you have something you wanted to speak with me about? Or were you just checking where we planned to rest for the night?"

He darted to her side, moving amazing quick for a boy of only six or seven summers. "Are you alone, Spirit Talker?"

"I'm never alone, Quanah. You should know that by now."

His eyes flickered up to the canopy of trees then to the path Kajika had taken. "I wanted to tell you something, but I didn't want anyone else to hear."

"All right."

Once again, Quanah glanced toward the place where she had last seen Kajika before his path had taken him out of her sight.

"If you're worried about Kajika, you should probably tell me whatever it you want to say. He won't be long."

That seemed to be all the prompting Quanah needed. "I saw something. The other day when your father's tepee was damaged."

She frowned. "What did you see?"

He looked down at his moccasins before answering. "It looked like a wolf."

Her heart skipped in her chest. "What kind of wolf?"

He shrugged. "A big dark one."

"Why should that need to be kept a secret? Chief Hiamovi already told us they thought some kind of wild animal had gotten in."

He shook his head. "I don't think it was a normal wolf."

"Why not?"

"Because it started walking on two legs just before it disappeared into the forest." He locked her straight in the eye. "Wolves don't do that."

She frowned. "No, they don't," she murmured.

"I tried to follow it, but I couldn't find where it had gone after it went into the trees."

She said a prayer of thanks that he hadn't been able to find the creature. The images of the blood left from the attack on Ghigau and the baby were still fresh in her mind. There was no telling what it might have done to Quanah.

"Why didn't you tell Chief Hiamovi?" she asked, even though she knew the answer.

Quanah pushed a rock with his foot. "I wasn't sure I had really seen it at first." Then he shrugged. "Then I didn't want anyone to think I was just making it up. Like Dichali. He's always making stuff up to scare the younger ones."

She nodded in understanding.

"But you believe me, don't you?"

The look in his eyes was earnest, and nothing he said had given her warning of an untruth. "I do."

His shoulders slumped in relief, but then he scrunched up his face. "You aren't going to tell Father, are you?"

"I can't promise that I never will, but no, I see no reason to alarm him at the moment."

Quanah pressed his lips together then nodded.

"Do you think you could show me and Kajika where the wolf, or whatever it was, went?"

"Yes." He cocked his head. "Are you going to track it?"

"No. She isn't."

At the sound of Kajika's voice, Quanah jumped as if he had been bitten.

Ahyoka smothered her grin. She was getting used to Kajika's nearly silent approach, but it was nice to know she wasn't the only one disturbed by it.

"Kajika, this is Quanah. He and his brothers stand watch around the village. He said he saw something the night Father's tepee was plundered." She waited until Kajika put their supplies down then tipped her head to Quanah. "Go ahead and tell him what you saw."

She watched Kajika's face as Quanah repeated his story. Other than the tensing of the muscle in his jaw and a quick glance in her direction, he gave no outward reaction.

"Where were you when this wolf left?" Kajika asked the boy.

"In a tree I like to use when I'm on that side of the village."

Kajika frowned. "How high had you climbed?"

Quanah pointed to one of the branches on a nearby tree. "About the same as that one."

"Was the creature walking away from you or passing from one side to the other in front of you?"

"Away from me."

"You're sure the shadows didn't play tricks on you? After all, your view from up there would have been different than if you were on level ground."

Quanah nodded. "I did wonder if I had gone a little moon touched at first. But, no, I'm certain it was only on two feet when it ran off."

"What makes you so certain?" Ahyoka asked.

"It stopped, right before the place where the trees clumped together. It looked as if it were doing something, but then it turned, threw whatever was in its hand off to the side closest to me, and took off into the woods."

Kajika uncrossed his arms. "Any idea what it threw?"

"No. Whatever it was, it wasn't very big. It didn't make much noise when it landed. I went back the next day but couldn't find anything. Even in the daylight."

Kajika and Ahyoka exchanged glances over the boy's head.

"It's too dark to see much now and Ahyoka needs to rest. Come by after the morning meal and show us where your tree is."

Quanah looked back and forth between them. "I'll come as soon I can get away from the little ones."

"Thank you, Quanah," Ahyoka said.

He tipped his head in acknowledgement. "I should get back to my watch now."

"Spread the word that I'll be on watch here. You and the others can mind the rest."

"But you're a guest," Quanah protested. "It would be ungracious of us—"

"He's a warrior first," Ahyoka softly reminded him. "Worry not. We are well protected here. Tell the others."

After a quick glance at Kajika, Quanah sprinted away, taking a different path than he had come.

Their eyes met and the fluttery sensation she always felt when he was near turned into a slow burn. Warmth spread through her body and pooled between her legs.

"I have to say that I'm surprised you didn't attempt to bathe on your own."

She smiled. "Someone told me it isn't a weakness to accept help when it's offered, especially when it's needed."

"Hmmm. You have a wise friend."

"Besides," she held her hands out to silently ask for his help getting up. "I—" Her breath caught in her throat when he scooped her up and held her against his chest. "I kind of liked it when you carried me here." Her cheeks warmed at her admission.

With a grunt, he glanced down at her then marched toward the stream.

She marveled at how easily he navigated the roots of the trees lining the river bank. Without stopping, he walked right into the water.

When the cool liquid touched her skin, she sucked in a breath and straightened her spine. "Oh. That's a little colder than I expected."

"Hold your breath."

"What?"

With no other warning, he ducked beneath the surface.

She sputtered as he lifted them out of the water. "Why did you do that?" She wiped her eyes with her free hand.

"You get used to the chill if you do it quickly."

"Yes, but you could have warned me."

"I did."

"Barely," she groused.

His lips twitched. "Did you get wet?"

"A little."

"Do I need to go under again?"

"No!" She flung her arm around his neck and tried to wiggle out of his grasp.

He laughed. "All right. Calm down."

She eased her choking hold on him. "You can put me down. My foot really isn't that bad."

His brows furrowed. "It's only been one day and you haven't rested much."

She patted his chest. "It's fine. But if it will make you feel better, I'll stay right next to you."

He slowly released his hold until she could stand.

She smiled up at him. "You didn't give me a chance to take off my dress. Much less dig out my bathing rub before we got in the water."

"Your what?"

"My bathing rub." She pulled her hair to one side and twisted the bundle to squeeze water out. "Would you mind getting it from my bag?"

"What is it for?"

"It's something I made to help clean my skin. I added a few

berries and sweetgrass to make it smell nice too."

He sloshed out of the creek and retrieved the pack. He held up a few bundles of linen and animal skins until she nodded he'd found the right one, then marched back to her side.

"Thank you." She opened the skin and scooped out a palm full of the paste then closed the pouch and looped the drawstring around her neck to keep it out of the water. After rubbing her hands together to spread the concoction over both palms, she offered one to Kajika for inspection. "Smell."

He took a quick sniff. "That is even better than the soap Winema gives me from time to time."

She smiled, pleased that he approved. "Turn around and I'll wash your back."

He seemed surprised by her offer but quickly complied.

Starting at the lower part of his back, she ran her hands all the way up, following the ridge in the center, then circled outward across his shoulders. The muscles beneath her fingers tensed then relaxed as he surrendered to her ministrations.

"Thank you for watching over me," she said quietly. "Other than my father or Maska, no one has stood up to Chief Hiamovi on my behalf."

"The men of your village are fools," he mumbled.

She chuckled. "Perhaps. I believe they fear what they do not understand. Sadly, no one seems inclined to make an effort to understand."

He grunted in response.

She focused on rubbing the slick paste across each shoulder and then down each arm. Having someone to tend to that wasn't ill was a nice change. And being able to touch the rippling muscles she had admired for the last four days was a dream come true.

"Let me get your chest," she suggested after doing all of the places she could reach that were above the water.

He slowly turned to face her. His voice dropped into a husky tone she had not heard before. "Do I get to use that on you also?"

"I, uh..." She looked at her coated hands then down at her damp dress.

"You'll have to take that off first."

Heat blossomed in her cheeks. "Perhaps I should finish washing you?"

"I can't promise to keep my hand off you while you do."

95

The heat in his gaze sent ripples of warmth through her body. She might be new to the things that went on between men and women, but she'd give almost anything to have him look at her this way until the sun and moon no longer crossed the horizon.

18

Those tiny hands of hers were going to be the death of him.

Even something as simple as washing away dust and dirt scattered his thoughts and made it hard to focus on anything except the way it had felt when their bodies joined. If a bear or an enemy were to walk up on them right now, he would likely not notice.

All the more reason he needed to find who or what had killed Dyami and return to his village.

She told him she had no expectation of becoming his or any man's wife and that he was free to leave once the killer had been found. But something warned him he'd never be able to forget her if he did leave her behind.

He would seek Yonaguska's council when he returned. Meanwhile, it couldn't hurt to steal one more moment with her. He wrapped his hands around her wrists and pulled them away from his chest.

A crease appeared between her brows as she looked up.

He dipped his head and touched his lips to hers. Despite his need to capture and plunder, he gentled his kiss, banking the embers of what could quickly become a raging fire. The idea that no other man had done the things they were doing pleased him more than it should. He wanted to show her all the ways they could pleasure each other.

If only he had enough time with her.

Pushing that thought aside, he skimmed his hands over her

back, looking for the laces to her dress. Once he'd loosened them, he pulled the clingy garment up and over her head. The wad of fabric landed with a sloppy thud on the rock he'd tossed it to.

When he looked down at her, he nearly swallowed his tongue. The raw beauty of her naked body captivated him. Why he had been given a chance to not only see her this way but to also touch her baffled him.

Her fingers danced across his belly and ribs. The expression on her face led him to believe she was as fascinated by him as he was of her. She leaned closer and pressed a kiss on the center of his chest. Without lifting her lips, she skimmed them up and over to one side until she reached his nipple.

When she sucked the tiny bud into her mouth, his breath caught. His hand fisted in her hair when she rolled her tongue over and around the now sensitive tip.

"I—" He hissed through his teeth when she dragged her teeth over it. "I still need to wash you."

She pulled back and gave him a shy smile. "All right."

"Can you give me some of your bathing rub?"

She loosened the pouch and scooped a bit out then wiped it onto his open palm. The fresh herbal scent wafted up to him as he rubbed his hands together.

He watched her face as he rubbed the mix across her skin. Despite the amount of time she spent in the sun, her skin felt soft. It wasn't due to a pampered lifestyle. From what he could see, her family worked hard for their people. Perhaps her herbs helped.

She tracked his touches, occasionally glancing up at him. Before long her eyes took on a heavy, sensual look and her body grew lax. When he had cleaned all of her exposed parts, he cupped water in his hands and let it slide down her body.

He couldn't resist leaning forward and licking a drop from her chest.

"Is there anything else you wish to wash?" he asked.

She blinked as if she didn't understand his question. "Um…no. I think you got all of the dust and the smell of horses off."

"Good." He scooped her up in his arms, making her squeak in alarm, and carried her to their sleeping mats. When she looked up at him in question, he kissed her.

Her enthusiastic response pleased him. He knew from the talk of the elders that not every woman enjoyed what went on between a man and woman. He wanted to make sure she didn't lose that feeling.

He lay her on the mat then knelt at her feet. His hands skimmed up her legs, parting them further as he went. He leaned in and pressed kisses against the bend of her knee. As he moved toward the juncture between her legs, he licked the remaining drops of water off.

The closer he moved to her center, the more she squirmed. He gently held her in place with one hand on her hip while he slowly ran his tongue over the folds of her core. Her movements stilled and she seemed to stop breathing.

It pleased him to be able to show her yet another form of pleasure. He savored his prize. Every lick and nibble he gave her was only for her pleasure. He pushed her right up to the brink three times until she whimpered with need.

"Kajika, please," she begged.

"Not just yet." He slipped one finger into her channel. His cock hardened further as he remembered how tightly she had fit around him yesterday. He still couldn't believe he had been the first man to lay with her. It stirred something primitive inside of him. A need to claim and protect her warred with the knowledge that he might not be able to.

He could, however, make her scream his name. And he planned to do just that.

He moved up and latched onto one of her breasts. As he teased the hardened peek with his lips and tongue, he continued to stimulate that sensitive bud between her legs.

She clutched at his back and her breath came in pants. Lifting her hips, she sought what only he could give her.

When he sensed she neared the edge again, he pulled away. She whimpered in protest.

He reached for her hips and turned her over so that she rested on her hands and knees. She shot a questioning look at him over her shoulder. In answer, he licked a trail up the center of her back. Her hiss of breath told him she had not broken free of his sensual web.

With one hand, he guided his cock to her opening. As he sank into her welcoming depths, he held her in place by her hip. He had to grit his teeth against the wash of pleasure and the urge to simply drive into her.

He went as far as he could then reached around her hip and found her sensitive bud between her legs. As soon as he touched her there she pushed back, deepening his invasion. It took every drop of control he had to remain focused on her pleasure.

He slid his cock back until it neared the end of her channel then sank all the way back in. He kept up the slow, steady pace even as he rubbed slow circles around her swollen bud. When she resisted his efforts to stay in place, he increased his efforts.

Her moans of pleasure were music to his ears. He drove her higher and higher, closer to that edge. Just when he worried he wouldn't be able to hold out, he felt her channel rippling over his cock. He pumped into her harder, determined to push her over.

Her cry of fulfillment and the rush of warmth around his cock sent him spiraling after her. They both collapsed onto the mat below them as they gasped for air.

They had been so caught up in each other that Kajika only now realized the sun had set. She curled up next to him and put her head on his chest. He could feel the pounding in her heart from where her chest pressed against his. He reached for the linen wrap she had left next to their mats and tossed it over them.

He dropped a kiss on the top of her head.

"Dream sweet," he whispered.

She yawned and snuggled closer. "You also."

As he lay beneath the canopy of trees and listened to the sounds of the nights, he wondered if perhaps this wasn't one of the reasons men returned home. This feeling of contentment. Of being with the one person who brought peace to your life.

As he drifted off to sleep, he decided the idea of taking a wife could indeed be worthwhile.

19

Morning light filtered through the leaves and roused Ahyoka from a surprisingly restful sleep. Her body was sore in a few new places, but something about waking in the arms of a man warmed her body and soul.

Kajika nuzzled the side of her neck, sending tiny bumps all the way down her leg. "Good morning," she murmured.

"Good morning."

The parts of her that were not toasty from the heat radiating off his body warmed at the sound of his husky voice.

"Did you sleep well?" he asked.

"I did. How about you?"

"Surprisingly so." He glanced at the trees surrounding them. "I actually don't remember ever sleeping so peacefully while away from my own tepee and sleeping mat. I can't decide if it's because you wore me out or if this really is a special place."

"It could be both."

He grinned down at her. "It could."

As they lay side by side and talked, her leg had crept over his and now came to rest hear his hip. He grabbed her calf and looked closer at her foot. "Is it any better today?"

"It isn't causing me pain, but I haven't put any weight on it yet."

He nodded. "How about if I catch a couple of fish for our breakfast then we'll wait for your little friend to return."

"Can you make it the way you did at the river yesterday? That was very good."

"As long as you still have some of those plants you added while it cooked."

"Oh, I have plenty of sweetgrass." She sat up then realized she had not put her dress back on before falling asleep. "I, uh…" She pulled her hair forward, covering her breasts as she looked for her clothes.

He fetched her discarded garment and brought it to her. "You have nothing to be embarrassed about with me. I could look at you all day and night."

The kiss he pressed against her lips fanned the flame within her again. There must be something wrong with her if she craved him so after the night they spent together.

"As much as I would like to stay here in your safe place with you, we cannot."

She nodded then pulled her dress over her head. "There's a berry bush just over there. I can gather some of those as well as a few nuts while you catch the fish."

"That will be good." He brushed his fingers across her check then headed to the river.

Her heart did a flip within her chest. She needed to be careful and not read too much into his actions. He would be leaving after they found the killer. He might be part of her destiny, but that didn't mean it would play out exactly the way she would like.

She lit a small fire and prepared a couple of tree branches for cooking their fare. In a short time, he returned with three fish large enough to provide a plentiful breakfast. They worked well together, almost intuitively knowing what the other needed. Despite their lack of conversation, it felt comfortable.

No sooner had they sat down to eat their meal than the young watcher returned.

"Did you eat, Quanah?" Ahyoka asked.

"Yes, but I'd gladly take a few of those berries off your hands." He grinned as only a boy who had been spared the cruelty of war and famine could.

Ahyoka handed Quanah a bowl with the food they hadn't eaten.

"I'm guessing the night watch passed without incident?" Kajika asked.

Quanah nodded after stuffing a handful of berries and nuts into his mouth.

Kajika stood then offered his hand to Ahyoka. He pulled her to her feet before steadying her. "Are you able to walk with us this morning? Your foot doesn't seem to be paining you much, but I don't want to strain or reinjure it."

"It's much better." She smiled. "Mother River sent her blessings to speed my healing." Her eyes twinkled. "I told you this was a special place."

"Very well. We should go." He waved toward the wooded area. "Quanah, can you take us to the place where you spotted the wolf?"

Quanah chatted happily as he led the way through a winding path only he could see. Eventually he stopped and pointed up into one of the trees. "That's my lookout spot."

Kajika tipped his head back and looked to where the boy pointed. "There aren't many low branches. You're able to climb that far without them?"

Quanah smiled proudly. "Mother says I climb better than a squirrel."

"I would say so," Kajika mumbled.

"The wolf thing walked from here." He gestured to their left. "To over there." The area he indicated had a dense tangle of shrubs and trees grown together.

Kajika looked to Ahyoka. "Do you see anything unusual?"

She glanced at Quanah. "Let me check." She turned away from them and called upon the land spirits to show her what couldn't be seen through normal vision.

Spirit Talker come see.
Evil walked this way.
We feared.
We hid.

Kajika moved behind her as if to protect her back.

Quanah watched from beneath his lookout tree without asking questions.

Something drew her attention near one of the trees. She followed the already fading trail toward the spot Quanah had pointed out. Her instincts screamed for her to stop a few paces away.

She looked at Kajika and told him in a lower tone, "I think it is the same person."

Kajika nodded, letting her know he'd heard. "Let's get back to the village. I wish to speak to Chief Hiamovi."

She held up her finger. "One more moment." She scanned the ground from left to right until she felt a pull off to one side.

"What are you looking for?"

"Quanah said he thought the wolf-man had thrown something in this direction. I want to know what." She took a few more steps then something in the leaves caught her eye. "There." She knelt to look closer.

Quanah followed, then leaned over her shoulder. "What is it?"

Ahyoka picked up a twig and pushed leaves around until she uncovered a beaded band. "That's Maska's."

"Are you sure?" Kajika asked.

She nodded. "Mother made it for him when he was a baby."

"Has it been harmed?" he asked.

She tipped her head to one side to change the angle of her vision. "Actually, no, I don't think so. I believe the protection charms she wove into the design still hold."

He handed her a piece of linen he pulled from his pouch. "Do you want to wrap it like you did the other things we've found?"

Taking the cloth from him, she let him see how much she appreciated his gesture. "Thank you." As soon as she finished wrapping Maska's bracelet, she stood and gave him a small smile. What she really wanted to do was throw her arms around him and kiss him soundly, but that would not be appropriate in front of Quanah.

"Now let's go see Chief Hiamovi," he said.

She nodded her consent.

Before they reached the main part of the village, Quanah scampered away to go find his brothers. She didn't blame him for not wanting to deal with Chief Hiamovi and promised to leave him out of their conversation unless they had no alternative.

"Your Chief won't believe it if we tell him there is a man who can change into a wolf and is the one who attacked your father's tepee," Kajika said softly as they made their way to the chief's tepee.

"No, he won't."

Kajika fell silent until they reached the outer ring of Chief Hiamovi's gathering place. "Let me handle this."

She frowned but nodded her agreement.

Kajika told the elder who tended the fire in the circle of their need to speak with the chief. The elder gestured for the young boy who played off to one side to go and get their leader.

A few minutes later, the chief came out and greeted Kajika. He barely even cast a glance in her direction. She shouldn't let his blatant dismissal bother her but sometimes it did. Especially when he did it in front of an honored guest.

He gestured for them to sit near his customary seat. As they did, a few of the village elders shuffled in, presumably to listen to the day's news.

"Ahyoka and I followed the trail of the one responsible for the damage to her father's tepee. I have reason to believe it may be the same person who attacked my cousin."

"It wasn't a wild animal?" the chief asked.

"No," Kajika told him.

"I was told a wolf had been spotted," Chief Hiamovi protested.

"Yes. I heard that also."

The chief puffed up. "But you don't believe our people?"

"I believe the man responsible for the attacks wants us to believe a wolf did these things."

"You mean someone pretended to be a wolf?" Disbelief laced the chief's voice.

"It is possible."

The chief put both of his beefy fists on his thighs and leaned forward. "How do you plan to prove it one way or the other?"

"By finding him," Kajika said. "I need to search the area to determine where this man may have gone."

"He could be hiding in the woods waiting to attack again," one of the elders cackled in alarm.

"We need to send for our warriors," another elder whined.

"A message has already been sent," the chief told them.

As they often did, the men argued about what should be done and how to best protect themselves. Before they came to any conclusion, the voices of the land rose up and drowned out their bickering. There were so many voices speaking at once that Ahyoka's couldn't make out anything they were saying.

Birds, trees, squirrels, ancestors, the wind. They all clamored for her attention and created a roar within her head. Beads of moisture broke out on her forehead and she struggled to build a protective wall around herself. She clasped her hands over her ears, trying to block out some of the noise, but it did little to help. The effort became too much and she sank to her knees in agony.

Kajika face appeared before her in a show of concern. His lips moved, but she couldn't hear what he said over the voices shouting in her head.

She shook her head and tried again to form some kind of protective shell.

Kajika grabbed her face with both hands and forced her to look him in the eye. As soon as she met his gaze, something clicked into place. The roar eased into a rumble and then into a murmur. Finally, she could focus on only one or two of the messages instead of the flood.

Her heart beat against her chest, but she didn't dare break her connection with Kajika. For some reason his presence made it possible for her to filter through the assault of information. He started to release her, but she grabbed his wrists to maintain the contact.

"What's wrong?"

"I…" She struggled to find the words even as she listened to what the spirits were telling her. "There's something wrong. Another attack."

"What's wrong with her?" Chief Hiamovi demanded. "What did she say?"

"Who was attacked?" Kajika ignored the chief and searched her face.

"I'm not sure." Her head pounded from the onslaught. Finally a name came to her. "Nitis." She sucked in a breath. "Nitis is in trouble. He's been attacked."

A collective gasp could be heard from those gathered nearby.

"Who is Nitis?" Kajika asked. No one offered an explanation. He adjusted her face, making her focus on him and his question. "Who is Nitis?"

"A, ah…" She blinked, trying to clear her thoughts. "He's the medicine man who inhabits the hills north of here." She struggled to her feet. "I have to find him."

"You cannot go wondering about the hills alone," the chief declared. "Not now that we know there have been attacks. Your father would never permit it."

"Then I'll ask Ouray or one of his brothers go with me," she countered.

"Our men are needed to protect the village, not chase after a girl and whatever crazy idea her latest vision told her to do." He jerked his chin in the direction of the village. "See to your duties and wait for your father and brother to return. Take it up with them if you still wish to see Nitis."

Ahyoka's lips pressed together. She was tired of having to keep her opinions to herself, and the chief kept making it difficult to do so.

The chief shook his head. "We don't even know if Nitis still lives. No one has seen him in several moons."

Kajika's expression darkened. "Is he not one of your people?"

"At one point he was, but he hasn't claimed us in many seasons," one of the elders explained.

"Does no one ever check on him?" Ice dripped from each of his words.

The chief pointed her way. "She and her brother do."

"Is there really no one who can go with her?"

"None that I am willing to spare." The chief's tone held finality.

Kajika stood. "Then it looks as if I'm heading north." He looked down at her. "Come. We need to prepare the horses and repack the supplies." Without a glance back, he walked out of the circle.

She blinked in surprise then hurried after him.

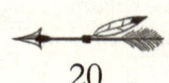

20

How did a man who thought and acted like an ass ever rise to be chief? No wonder Ahyoka frequently wandered away from her village. Chief Hiamovi's attitude about her had infected nearly everyone around them.

Ahyoka caught up to him. "Did you really mean it?"

"Mean what?" He kept marching toward the river.

"That you would go with me to find Nitis."

"Yes, I did."

She grabbed his arm to slow his pace. "You don't have to. I know you want to look for the wolf-man for your cousin's sake. I don't want to keep you from doing that."

He came to a stop. "Yes, I do want to look for the one responsible for Dyami's death. I assume you have an explanation for your near collapse and a reason for suddenly wanting to go see this medicine man friend of yours. That you aren't just dropping in to check on his well-being."

"I, uh…" She glanced at the villagers they passed then lowered her voice. "I believe Nitis has been attacked and may be gravely injured."

"How do you know this?"

She bit her lip. "I told you I hear things. I receive messages from the spirits. They warn me of things."

He nodded.

"This time they brought me a message. A very insistent message from Nitis. He needs my help. I believe he may be dying. I think he was attacked."

"Do you think it was the creature that attacked us?"

"I don't know. It's possible. Especially if this skinwalker is interested in those with the blood of a shaman."

"Even more reason I should go with you. Besides, I made a promise to my chief that I would keep you safe. I have seen no one in this village I would trust to do so in my place. Until your father or brother return, you have my protection."

"Thank you."

Something about her expression touched him, made him feel as if he could take on the biggest bear in the woods and come away victorious. "You're welcome." He gestured toward their things. "Where do we find Nitis?"

"His home is less than a day's ride on horseback. But I'm not certain he was attacked at home." They each set about repacking their supplies. "His magic is strong. His home is well protected by the spirits. It is more likely he was attacked while hunting or walking about the land."

Kajika paused. "But you can find him, right?"

"Yes."

She looked as if she were waiting for him to say something, but he didn't know what so he returned to his task. "Other than water for our journey, is there anything else you need to take?"

"I need to empty some of the grasses I gathered along the way from my pouch and replenish my herbs. It will only take a moment though."

True to her word, Ahyoka returned before he had even finished filling the water skins. They readied the horses and set off. Even though she had explained where they needed to go, he was content to let her lead the way.

Like the journey to her village, they rode side by side, mostly in silence. He remained alert to potential threats while she listened to the voices of the animals and the land and let them be their guide. It felt unnatural to follow a trail he could not see, but until she proved herself wrong, he would wait and watch. Oddly, just being with her, offering his protection whether she needed it or not, seemed right.

As his thoughts churned in his head, he realized she had stopped.

He turned his horse so he could see what had caught her

attention. "What's wrong?"

She climbed down from her mount and crept toward a thicket of brush. "I'm not sure. I thought I heard something."

He nudged his horse forward as he pulled his bow from where it hung on his saddle. What was wrong with him that he lost focus so easily? "What did you hear?"

"It was just the rustling of leaves and branches. But I thought I heard a growl too." She held up one hand to stop him when he reached for an arrow. "Not an aggressive growl."

"What are your animal friends telling you?"

"Nothing." She finally looked up at him. "That's why I don't believe there is any threat to us."

No sooner had the words left her lips than two bear cubs burst through the foliage and rolled in their direction. The cubs were so tangled in their play they didn't notice them right away.

Ahyoka grinned at the bears' antics. Kajika quickly scanned the surrounding trees then pinned his eyes on the brush the cubs has fallen through.

"Get on your horse," he told her.

"Why? They won't harm us."

"They won't but their mother will if she finds us near them."

"I hadn't thought of that."

"Move slowly and quietly but get on your horse."

This time she did as he said. Before she could even get her one leg over the horse's back, the brush crashed and snapped and a large brown bear lumbered into the light. It lifted its head and sniffed the area. Her sights landed on her cubs then Ahyoka and him.

The mother bear let out a growl that stopped all of them in their tracks.

"Get. On. Your. Horse." His teeth were gritted as he snapped out the command.

Instead of doing as he said, she pushed her horse in his direction, effectively blocking him from notching an arrow with the bear in sight.

"What are you—"

"Mother bear, we mean you no harm," she called out. As she spoke, her voice took on a strange tone. It became lighter, yet resonated through his body. The hair on his neck stood on end. "The Great Spirit has blessed you with two strong babies. Please know that we honor their life as well as your own."

The bear made a yowling sound as if to answer Ahyoka.

He nudged his horse to the side so he could see what was happening while Ahyoka's danced nervously next to him.

"We seek only to pass through these lands to find the one who inhabits the hill," she told the mother.

The bear yowled again in response.

"With your permission, we will be on our way."

Kajika's mouth fell open when the bear dipped its head in a sort of bow to Ahyoka. He sat in stunned silence as the bear ambled over to its cubs and nudged them toward the woods once more.

Ahyoka reached for her horse's reins while Kajika remained rooted to the spot.

"We should go," she told him.

"That was very…"

"Odd?"

"Did that bear speak to you?"

"Yes." She climbed up onto her horse. "We really should go now."

"Is she coming back?"

Ahyoka looked in the direction the bear had wondered off. "Unlikely. But we've lingered too long here."

"You're right." He reattached his bow then took up the reins. "Lead on." With one last glance behind them, he followed her to the base of the looming hills.

There was no mistaking what he had just seen. But if she could really talk to animals, what else might she be capable of?

21

Ahyoka's senses went on alert as soon as they reached the hills. She felt the warmth of Nitis's protection spells, but she also detected a cold prickling. Had something been chipping away at his charms? Even the land's energies that were normally rich and full in the hills had been dulled somehow.

"Something has been here," she cautioned Kajika.

"Animal, man, or something else?" he asked.

"I suspect something else."

She nudged her horse forward, encouraging it to cross the narrow stream. With more than just her ears, she listened to all that the Corn Mother had to say. She and Kajika both passed through Nitis's protective barrier with no problems. When they reached the other side of the stream, he stopped and looked back.

"Why does the air feel lighter on this side?" he asked.

"You feel a difference?"

"Yes, don't you?"

"Of course, but I'm surprised you noticed anything. Most people don't sense those kinds of things. They usually only feel either a draw or resistance to the area." She tipped her head to one side. "You seem to have a unique sensitivity to the land's energies."

"I figured you were just rubbing off on me."

A grin tugged at her lips. "Maybe so, Warrior. Maybe so." She led him to the path that would take them to Nitis's cave. Because of the narrow width, they were forced to ride one in front of the other.

When they reached the top, they navigated their way to the entrance of Nitis's cave. She dismounted and left her horse by the cluster of trees near the mouth of his cave. Kajika followed suit.

For there to be so many trees and brush in the area, it was unusually quiet. He expected to hear at least a few bird calls or other signs of life. Instead he heard almost nothing. Not even the rustling of leaves.

"I don't think he's here, but I'm going to check inside to be sure," Ahyoka said.

Kajika nodded but couldn't pull his gaze away from the surrounding trees. He couldn't shake the feeling that something was out there. Waiting for them.

Ahyoka emerged from the cave a moment later, shaking her head. "He's not there. His fire is cold, so he has been away for at least a couple of days."

"Any idea where he would have gone?"

"Not with certainty, but I can ask."

"I suggest that you do. Something tells me we're not alone."

So he picked up on that also. Kajika's senses were more in tune to the spirits' warnings than he would probably ever admit. She wasn't about to point it out. She closed her eyes and pulled on the flow of land's energy then sent her request out. Since they were standing on sacred ground, she received a response almost immediately.

Hurry, Spirit Talker.

The ancient one needs you.

Go with speed.

Go with care.

The evil one walks nearby.

An image of the stream that flowed on the other side of the hill popped into her mind. She felt certain they would find Nitis there.

"I think I know where he is." She went to her horse to retrieve her satchel. "Bring your bow and your knife."

"Where is he?"

"I was shown a spot next to the stream that runs along that side of the hill." She pointed in the direction she meant.

Without question, Kajika gathered the things she had suggested. She blinked in surprise. He hadn't mocked her or questioned why. That unsettled her more than the thought of facing the skinwalker again.

"Are we going?" he asked.

She shook off her thoughts. "Yes." She led him to a trail that ran along the side of the cave. "This is the most direct path to the stream, but it is a little narrow in places."

"If there aren't many branches from this main path, I'd rather go first," he said as he slipped his bow over his head and settled it across his chest.

"There aren't." She gestured for him to go ahead of her.

He pulled his knife from its sheath and gripped it in his hand, ready to strike if necessary. This time, she was glad he had it.

They navigated the trail quickly but quietly. His ability to move almost silently still amazed her. Next to him, she felt like a wild hog trampling through the underbrush.

When they neared the stream, Kajika paused and signaled for her to be still. They both scanned the area, looking for, well, anything. A hint of malice hung in the air. The need for caution warred with a growing sense of urgency.

"There." Kajika pointed to a boulder not far from the water's edge. Sticking out from behind the boulder she saw a pair of legs, but the main part of the body was hidden from view.

"Do you think it's safe?" she whispered.

"You'd know better than me," he mumbled.

Hurry, Spirit Talker.

Hurry.

"I'm going." She brushed past Kajika and hurried to see who lay on the ground. Kajika cursed under his breath then followed right behind her.

When Ahyoka rounded the boulder, her fears were confirmed. Nitis lay on the ground either asleep or dead. His clothes were ripped and torn and a pool of blood had formed beneath his back. Her fingers trembled as she reached for Nitis to see if he still lived. He felt cool, but not cold. When she rolled him onto his back, he let out a groan.

Kajika took up position behind her, once again protecting her back. "Is that Nitis?"

"Yes. And thankfully, he's still alive." She pushed Nitis's multi-colored blanket aside so she could look at his injuries. His linen shirt had been shredded from the number of cuts and scratches he'd received. It took little effort to rip the pieces of fabric away so she could better see.

Most of his injuries were minor, but the one that ran from his belly to his side worried her. His pants were caked with dried blood. She prayed he hadn't lost too much before they arrived.

She pulled a clean strip of linen from her satchel and pressed it against the wound. Nitis stirred and moaned when she applied pressure against his side.

"Can you tell what happened to him?" Kajika asked.

"My first guess would be that an animal of some kind attacked him." She glanced at Kajika. "But we have both seen that before with much worse results."

"I'm going to look around and see if I can figure out what might have done this. Are your spirits telling you anything?"

She stopped for a moment to focus on the pull from the land then shook her head. "They're quiet."

"Is that a good thing or a bad thing?"

"If we were in danger, they would tell me." She continued to check Nitis for injuries. "We are on sacred ground too. Unless this skinwalker is far more skilled than Nitis, his protections should aid us."

"I won't go far."

Even though her back was to him, Ahyoka sensed Kajika's presence wherever he went. She rummaged through her bag until she found the herbs she needed. Once she prepared them the way she wanted, she located the small bowl she always carried with her.

"Kajika?" she called out to get his attention. "Would you mind filling this with water?"

Without complaint, he retrieved the bowl she held out for him then headed to the stream. She had just returned to her task when the birds and insects went silent. She scanned the area around them, looking for the disturbance. Almost immediately a rumbling growl echoed across the open area.

Kajika dropped the bowl and reached for his bow. In a flash, he had an arrow notched and aimed in the direction the sound had come from.

The dried plants she had been holding fell from her hands as she scrambled to her feet. "Don't cross the stream," she warned Kajika as she rushed to his side. "Whatever it is should not be able to harm us here."

"That small span of water is not going to stop a wolf or a bear." He pulled back on the arrow, adding more tension to the bowstring.

"Help me get Nitis back to the cave." Ahyoka put her hand on his shoulder. "Believe me. Nothing with evil intent can reach us."

Another growl rumbled across the span, as if to disprove her words.

Kajika hesitated but finally gave in and lowered his bow. "Your friend needs to come first."

"Thank you."

They both rushed back to Nitis.

"I thought I'd bind the wound on his side before we tried to move him, but I think the other cuts can wait until we get him to the cave."

"Are you certain he can be moved?"

"Fairly certain." She pointed to Nitis's side. "I think this is the worst."

"Why is he not awake?" he asked.

"It's possible he hit his head on something, but I didn't notice any bumps or scrapes there. I suspect it's because he's weary and bled too much before we arrived. He may have simply grown tired after fighting off whatever did this to him."

Kajika nodded. "Can he be carried? Or should I make a pallet to pull him?"

"It would take time to gather branches and make a pallet. Unless you think he's too heavy to carry?"

"I've carried deer that weigh more than him. It won't be a problem."

"Let me make a paste of these." She held up the dried plants she'd dropped earlier. "I want to wrap his middle section before we go." She checked the area for her supplies. "What happened to the bowl I gave you earlier?"

Kajika grimaced. "I must have dropped it. I'll go get it."

Nitis stirred and opened his eyes.

"There you are." Ahyoka smiled and grasped his hand. "How are you feeling?"

"Not good." He tried to sit up, but she pushed him back down with little effort.

"You've been hurt. I'm not sure it's a good idea for you to move around yet."

Nitis looked from her to Kajika. He blinked in confusion. "I see you've found your spirit guardian already?"

"My what?" she asked.

Nitis pointed at Kajika. "Your guardian."

"That is Kajika. We were tracking who or whatever killed Kajika's cousin when I received word that you needed me. He agreed to keep me safe until Father and Maska return from the hunt, but he isn't my guardian."

Nitis patted her hand. "We'll see. I'm glad you were listening when I sent out the call. I knew I wouldn't make it much further."

A growl echoed through the area. Kajika had frozen where he knelt next to the stream. Across the narrow span, a black wolf bared its teeth at him. Kajika slowly lowered the bowl and reached for his knife. The closer his hand got to his weapon, the more the wolf snarled.

The dark beast moved closer to the water's edge. Ahyoka's mouth fell open as the beast stepped into the water.

"Get back, Kajika," she yelled.

"Give me my staff," Nitis ordered as he struggled to sit up.

Ahyoka's attention bounced from Kajika to Nitis and back again. Torn between the urge to rush to Kajika's side and do as Nitis bid, she blindly reached for Nitis's staff.

"Hand it to me now," Nitis's power-laced command pushed her into action.

She grabbed the staff and rushed to deliver it to Nitis.

"Leave this place," Nitis bellowed as soon as his hand wrapped around the wood. "This is holy ground. You shall not defile it with your evil." He slammed the end of his staff into the ground. "Be gone!"

The power of his words rippled across Ahyoka's skin and the ground trembled beneath her feet.

The beast snarled in response.

Kajika looked back at Ahyoka in question. Before she could answer him, a thundering rumble drew their attention to the west. The stream receded to a narrow band just before a furious rush of water slammed through the shallow bed.

The beast and Kajika both leapt away from the swelling tide onto their respective banks.

The beast roared out as if to tell them it wasn't finished with them, then turned and ran into the dark of the surrounding foliage.

Ahyoka's heart beat against her chest like a drum. She had never seen such a display of raw power. If she had been left speechless, what did Kajika think? Would he pack his things and run back to his village? He wasn't a coward, but things like this were often more than most people could understand, much less accept.

22

Ahyoka knelt beside Nitis. "Are you all right?"

He grasped his side. "A little sore."

Kajika flicked his thumb toward the place where the beast ran into the trees. "Is that what attacked you?"

Nitis grimaced. "Yes. I thought it was a wolf at first."

"But it isn't, is it?"

Nitis shook his head and pressed the bandage Ahyoka handed him against his side. "No. It was a deceiver. A skinwalker." He pulled the bandage away, looked at it, then put it back in place. The bandage was red but not soaked.

"Do you want a fresh one?" Ahyoka asked Nitis.

"No."

"Are you certain it was a skinwalker?" Kajika asked.

"Yes," Nitis told him. "I've only run across a few in my lifetime, but they are nearly impossible to forget."

Ahyoka and Kajika exchanged glances.

"So they aren't very common then?" Kajika pressed.

"No, they aren't, thank the Great Spirit." Nitis's voice sounded weary.

"I think we should take you back to your cave. Do you think you can withstand the move?" Ahyoka asked.

"I don't think I can walk that far, even if both of you help me."

"I will carry you," Kajika told him. "But I'm afraid it will then fall to you to keep watch for attack from behind."

"We are protected here," Nitis told him. "You have no need to worry about an attack."

Kajika's brow rose in question.

"This is sacred ground," Ahyoka explained.

"But weren't you attacked on sacred ground?" Kajika asked.

Nitis shook his head. "I was on the other side of the stream. I managed to get away and cross the boundary."

"The whole hill is protected. The stream marks one edge," Ahyoka added.

"So the skinwalker shouldn't have been able to cross that narrow span of water?" Kajika asked.

"No, it shouldn't have," Ahyoka said but looked to Nitis in question.

Nitis grimaced. "You're right. It shouldn't have been able to. If I hadn't strengthened the protections, I worry it might have."

Kajika glanced from one to the other. "So can it or can't it?"

Nitis met Ahyoka's gaze. "If it can, there would be nothing either of us could do to stop it."

Ahyoka's eyes widened in alarm.

"Well, then we should get you back to the cave before the sun sets," Kajika declared. He looked at Ahyoka. "And you will just have to keep an eye out while we make our way up the hill."

Ahyoka nodded. "Let me bind his side before you try to move him. Hopefully that will keep it from bleeding much more."

She worked quickly to secure his injury then Kajika shifted Nitis in his arms until they were both satisfied they could withstand the movement required to make it up the hill. Nitis's white hair cascaded over the multi-colored blanket Ahyoka had re-wrapped around his thin shoulders. His pants and fur-lined boots were dirty and blood splattered. If it weren't for his injuries, Kajika would wager the old man was healthy and strong. Nitis might not be able to walk far right now, but Kajika doubted he would be down long.

Once they began their ascent, Nitis said, "Ahyoka told me you are one of Yonaguska's people."

"I am."

"I remember Yonaguska," Nitis said. "He was Oconostota's oldest, wasn't he?"

"That's correct," Kajika said.

"A strong young man. Much like yourself, I suspect." He pushed a low-hanging branch aside. "I haven't travelled that way for many seasons. How do your people fare?"

"Our fields and hunts have provided more than enough for us. And normally the children play freely and the women are content."

"Normally? But not always?" Nitis asked.

Kajika gritted his teeth before answering. "We lost one of our newest families recently. My cousin, his wife, and their child. They were attacked in their own tepee, and it has made many of our people afraid."

"Something like that would," Nitis said. "Is that what led you away from home?"

"I seek the one responsible for the deaths."

"What have you learned?"

"We think the skinwalker we met at the river is the one we seek."

"You may be right." Nitis's expression turned pensive. "The spirits have been restless of late. I had wondered what disturbed them. The spirits told me something walked the land that should not. Our ancestors cry out for justice and mercy."

Kajika gritted his teeth. "I hope to give them that before long."

Nitis fell silent and eventually nodded off. When they reached the top of the hill, Ahyoka led them to a large stone near the cave entrance. "You can set him there," she suggested.

Even in the dim light, he could tell the area had been cleared to be used for sitting or perhaps working in the shade.

"It will be dark inside. I'll have to light a torch until we can get the main fire going. Why don't you rest with Nitis?" she suggested.

"I can light the torch," Kajika told her.

"I know you can, but you've just carried him all the way up the hill. I think you're entitled to take a moment. Besides, I know where everything is almost by feel."

He nodded his agreement.

"You are a strong warrior to have made it all this way without complaint." Nitis's voice sounded weaker than it had earlier.

With a shrug Kajika told him, "You are no heavier than the bucks we usually hunt."

Nitis chuckled. "I suppose that's better than a scrawny fawn."

Kajika's lip twitched. "Perhaps."

As he waited for Ahyoka to return, Kajika watched the last of the light fade into dark. Despite being unfamiliar with the area and knowing there was at least one predator out there, he felt oddly at ease. Was it because this was protected land? And what exactly protected the area? It couldn't be Nitis. The frail old man couldn't stand up to a rabbit right now, much less a bear or wolf.

Ahyoka turned the corner. The torch she held bathed the small area in flickering firelight. "Can you bring him inside?"

"Yes." Kajika tried to avoid waking Nitis as he picked him up again. He followed Ahyoka into the cave, but as they passed through the entrance, Nitis stirred. Perhaps the odd prickling sensation Kajika felt on his arms and legs disturbed Nitis as well.

"Why don't you lay him on his furs next to the firepit?" Ahyoka showed him the place she meant. She secured the torch in a holder on the wall. "I'll gather some wood while you rest." Before she left she handed both of them skins with water.

Kajika took a seat next to where Nitis lay. When he lifted his hand to drink from the pouch, his arm shook from the strain of the weight he'd carried. He took solace in knowing the weakness wouldn't last long. In four gulps, he drank most of the water he'd been given.

His gaze wandered to the entrance where Ahyoka had disappeared through. He didn't like her wandering out there alone in the dark. But he knew she was right. He needed a moment of rest and she would know better where to find things in the dark. And the reality was that it probably wasn't the first time she'd been alone in the dark. He suspected she'd been mostly alone for many seasons. He hated that thought.

"Why do you fear her?"

Kajika didn't bother pretending not to know who Nitis referred to. "She believes things I cannot."

"Have you tried?"

"Not as much as I could."

Nitis grunted.

"Why do you live up here away from the safety of the village?" Kajika countered.

The old man slowly rolled onto his side before answering. "After Adsila died, that was Ahyoka's mother," Nitis clarified, "I answered Hiamovi's summons to help his people. I stayed until I was called away. For some time now, it's been another's responsibility, but they have been reluctant to take their rightful place."

Kajika's heart twisted. "Ahyoka."

"She is a skilled healer and the spirits have spoken freely with her since she was a child." He lifted his chin as if listening to something on the wind. "She is more than capable of taking on the role as the village healer, but no. Her destiny lies elsewhere."

Kajika blinked in surprise. "Does she know that?"

"She does."

"Is that why Chief Hiamovi treats her as a burden more than a member of his tribe?"

Nitis lifted his head. "You saw that?"

"I did. And I didn't care for it."

"I've spoken with Paco and Hiamovi about it but nothing changed. If anything, I made it worse for her. I came to believe that it's the Great Spirit's way to make it easier for Ahyoka to accept her fate. When her times comes."

"You mean she is going to be forced to leave her family?"

"She will be forced to choose. As I said, her destiny lies elsewhere. It's up to her to follow it."

Kajika fell silent as he contemplated what he'd learned. If Ahyoka didn't have a place in her village, why did she stay? Because of her father and brother? Chief Hiamovi had made it clear that he didn't have a use for her. Many of the villagers followed the chief's example. It had to be an uncomfortable life given how often her father and brother left with hunting parties.

But where would she go? It wasn't safe for a woman to wander the countryside. Women needed family and the safety of a village to survive.

Would she consider living among Yonaguska's people? And why did the idea that she might calm some of the ill feelings that had been churning in his gut?

23

"Your wood pile is low," Ahyoka said when she returned. "I'll let Maska know he needs to work on it before winter."

"There is plenty of time before I'll need it," Nitis assured her.

She piled the small logs she gathered in the stone circle. Kajika leaned in to stack them so they would light faster.

"I'm sure Maska will come after he and Father return from their hunt."

"You and your brother are both good to his old man," Nitis murmured.

Ahyoka knelt beside Nitis. "We need to get you cleaned up so I can put some salve on your injuries."

Nitis waved a hand at her. "Bah."

"That cut on your side needs tending." She pointed at Nitis's middle. "I wasn't able to do more than wrap a couple of linens around it."

"I'm fine," Nitis insisted.

She looked to Kajika and silently pleaded for help.

"If that wolf-thing got anywhere near you, I would think you'd want to wash the smell off." Kajika shuddered in an exaggerated fashion. "I couldn't wait to jump in the river after I wrestled with it."

Nitis sighed. "Very well."

Ahyoka smiled her thanks at Kajika while he worked to light the main fire. Once the flame was strong enough, she put a basin of water on to heat so that Nitis wouldn't get chilled while he washed.

Then she and Kajika worked together to find something they could all eat for the last meal.

"I'll hunt for a few birds or rabbits in the morning so he has something easy to prepare for the next couple of days," Kajika offered.

"Thank you." She tossed a look in Nitis's direction. "He's a survivor, but I worry this injury took more out of him than he realizes."

"He probably does realize. Either way, I suspect he's stubborn enough to put on a brave front," Kajika suggested.

"You're right," she said with a sigh. "Even if you weren't here, he wouldn't tolerate me coddling him. He'll kick us out of here after he gets on his feet tomorrow."

"Will he be able to manage on his own?"

"I think so. He has for many seasons. And like you said, he's stubborn. Stubborn enough to force his way through any illness he does get. The only thing I can do is make sure he has the things he needs to survive for a few days within easy reach before we leave."

"All right. Let me know what I can do to help."

"I'll know better in the morning when I have the light again. Tonight I think the best thing we could all do is rest."

"You're probably right." He leaned in and whispered in her ear. "We may not be able to share a sleeping mat the way I'd like, but I am not giving up my place beside you just yet."

Her cheeks grew warm. "I am afraid I am becoming used to having you nearby."

He reached for the braid she had woven along one side of her hair. She felt the slide of his fingers along the knots as if they were skimming across her skin. When he reached the end, his hand dropped away but their eyes still held. He wore an unreadable expression, yet something passed between them.

An understanding of some kind.

Whatever connected them and drew them together time and again was real. But it would have to wait until this thing was done.

There would be time.

Later.

"If you think the water is warm enough, I will help Nitis scrub away the dirt and smell of the wolf," he suggested.

Ahyoka nodded then watched him rejoin Nitis near the fire. She remained in the deeper part of the cave where the food and other things were stored. As soon as he left, she registered the cool dampness of the cave. Funny how she hadn't noticed it while Kajika had been near.

As she normally did when she visited, she went through Nitis's storage jars, checking to see what he might need more of. She lingered long enough to give Nitis time for privacy; something sorely lacking in a cavern, even one as spacious as this. She might be a healer, but not everyone was comfortable disrobing around other people.

When she could hear Nitis and Kajika speaking freely, she took her small torch and the things she'd gathered for their meal and returned to where they had settled next to the fire. "It didn't look as if you had run out of anything yet." She gestured to the storage area she'd just left.

"Going through my things again?" Nitis groused.

"Of course." They had the same discussion every time she visited, but he seemed to feel the need to fuss. "Did I overlook anything or is there something I should have Maska bring when he comes?"

"No." Nitis pulled a clean blanket around his shoulders. "This has been a generous growing season. I gathered the few things I needed from that patch you planted or while out on one of my many walks."

"Good."

Ahyoka set bowls of fruit, nuts, and dried meat near the fire then handed each of the men several flat pieces of bread before taking her place on the other side of Nitis. Once she was situated, Nitis lifted his chin and gave thanks to the spirits. He also lifted his bowl in thanks to Ahyoka, doing the same to Kajika after.

Ahyoka murmured her thanks to the Great Spirit. Kajika surprised her by slightly lifting his bowl in acknowledgement instead of blatantly ignoring them.

"Tell me about your travels and how you came to find each other," Nitis prompted as they ate.

Ahyoka related the events of the last few days. Kajika filled in the places she had forgotten or hadn't seen. Finally, she pulled one of the linen-wrapped bundles from her satchel. "We found this in his cousin's tepee. I sensed a great deal of hostility from it, so I thought I'd keep it until we found out where it came from." She set the bundle in front of Nitis and let the corners of the linen fall open.

Nitis leaned closer and looked at the bit of animal pelt then reared back. "You haven't touched it have you?"

"No," Ahyoka reassured him. "I wrapped it in scraps of cloth so we wouldn't have to."

"I believe that came from the wolf we saw earlier." His face scrunched up. "It has definitely been tainted by dark magic."

Ahyoka nodded. "I sensed that."

"Hand me that middle jar." Nitis pointed to a row of clay jars that had been lined up against the base of the wall. Kajika retrieved the one he'd asked for then took his seat again. Nitis tossed a handful of herbs he pulled from the jar on to the skin then added a pinch of ash from the fire pit. When he touched a twig with a glowing ember to the skin, it exploded into a green flame.

"Our wolf is indeed a skinwalker."

Ahyoka grimaced. "I suspected but couldn't be certain. I've never encountered one before and didn't want to make a false claim."

"Your abilities have grown, Little Bird, you should be confident of them," Nitis mumbled as he pushed the charred remains of the linen and skin into the fire with a twig.

"We believe the same man attacked her father's tepee while she visited my village," Kajika added.

Nitis gaze leapt to her. "Your father's tepee?"

"Yes."

"What did they do to it?"

"We're not certain of everything," Kajika told him. "Things were overturned."

"It looked as if our things had been searched," Ahyoka added.

Nitis's frown deepened.

"We know it wasn't a wild animal or someone looking for food. Both times the dried meats were left undisturbed."

Ahyoka reached for her satchel and pulled out the other wrapped linen. "We found this in the woods not far from where that wolf had been. Someone saw the skinwalker throwing it away." Like the bit of fur, she set it in front of Nitis and let the linen corners fall open.

Nitis leaned closer. "That is familiar."

"It's Maska's. Mother made it for him."

"Ah." He held one hand over the bracelet, closed his eyes and chanted below his breath. When he opened his eyes, he told her, "The blessings held. Her protection remains in place." He folded the linen around the piece and handed it back to her. "It may have been mishandled, but it can be cleansed. Wait until the next storm and ask for their help to wash away the stain."

"That is what I had planned to do," she assured him.

"Their?" Kajika asked.

"The spirits of our ancestors," Ahyoka explained. "Many people can see and feel them in the form of storms because they are at their strongest. During these times, they are usually open to lending their aid."

Kajika tipped his head in understanding.

"Now, tell me what you know about this killer," Nitis prompted.

They told him everything they had seen or been told. Ahyoka described the unpleasant feelings she'd experienced whenever she had been close to the places the killer had been.

Nitis tossed a few herbs into the fire and looked deep into the flames. After a moment, Kajika glanced her way in question. She shook her head to let him know he shouldn't disturb Nitis's concentration.

Finally Nitis lifted his head. "Many shadows follow this thing. Much has been hidden from me. I sense anger. Much anger. A need for vengeance."

"Mine?" Kajika asked.

"No. Your feelings, while strong, come from love and a need for justice. The winds carry the scent of rot. I believe this person was once wronged and they let that pain turn into hatred, and now they are rotting from the inside out."

"What does that have to do with Dyami? Or of his innocent child? I cannot believe they did anything to wrong someone so much they would want to kill them."

Nitis's eyes clouded over, turning a milky white color. His voice deepened. "No. They were innocent of any wrong doing. The one you seek interfered with their lives and their destinies in order to gain power. Their spirits have been used to fuel the darkness growing inside of this skinwalker."

Ahyoka shivered.

"You must find the one responsible. They must pay for their crimes before they grow stronger. If they continue unchecked, the people of this land will weep tears of blood." Nitis slumped forward as if he had suddenly been released by an unseen force.

Kajika reached for Nitis, but Ahyoka stopped him with a hand gesture. "Nitis? Are you all right?" she asked.

Nitis's chest expanded and collapsed as he took short, choppy breaths.

"Nitis?" she asked again

"I'm fine." His voice sounded raspy and he continued to gasp for air.

"You need rest to heal," Ahyoka told him. "You should not have made yourself even more weary over this."

Nitis sat up straight then inhaled deeply through his nose and let it out slowly. When he opened his eyes, they were free of the cloudy haze. Ahyoka handed him a cup. Nitis drank deeply and cleared his throat.

"The one you seek is near," Nitis told them. "You must find him."

"Kajika can track just about anything. Since we know this skinwalker has been near the river, I'm sure he will be able to find it again," Ahyoka told him.

"I fear, if you do not stop it, the next death will give them what they seek."

"What do they seek?" Kajika asked.

"Power."

"From the spirits they take," Ahyoka whispered. How could someone do that? Kill innocent people to make yourself more of something?

"But how does the spirits of people he's killed give him power?" Kajika asked.

Nitis picked up a stick and drew a symbol in the ash that circled the fire pit. "My grandmother told me about skinwalkers. Her people believe them to be medicine men or witches who went too far with their abilities. Those who dared to dabble with dark magic."

Kajika raised his brow in question.

Nitis added, "Things better left untouched. Most skinwalkers become greedy and vain and stop using their power to help their people. Instead they focus on gaining wealth or pursuing the man or woman they desire, no matter the consequences. They become less human, more the animal they change into."

"You think this man is killing people in order to make himself strong enough to seek vengeance on someone else?"

"Or a group of people." He cocked his head and looked off into the distance. "Their own tribe, perhaps."

"But why?" Ahyoka asked.

Nitis shook his head. "That I cannot answer."

24

The next morning, Kajika rose as soon as the sun began to lighten the dark. He whispered to Ahyoka that he would return as soon as he'd caught a few things for Nitis to eat.

He circled Nitis's mountain twice before even drawing his bow to begin his hunt. The first pass he made near the top, the second near the base. Each time he drew close to what he suspected to be the border of Nitis's land, he felt a prickling on his arms and neck.

After the unusual things he'd seen while traveling with Ahyoka, it would probably be best to remain on the inside of that border. Just in case.

He turned to make his way back up the hill but then noticed a fresh set of foot prints in the soft ground near the invisible boundary. It was possible Nitis had made them, but they were smaller than he expected them to be. He followed them until they changed from man to beast. When they did, he stopped and studied them as well as everything about the area.

The length between each print did not change between steps. Even after the man's disappeared. It looked as if the beast walked on two legs. At least for a time.

He couldn't be certain from where he crouched, but the prints seemed to change again when they turned and led away from Nitis's hill. As if the creature dropped to all fours and increased his pace.

He wanted to give chase, but he couldn't risk leaving Ahyoka unprotected. If something were to happen to him while chasing an unknown, she would be forced to travel home alone. That he couldn't allow.

To turn his mind away from that which he could do nothing about, he looked for tracks and other clues of animals he could easily catch. His search led him to an unusual circle of stones. In the middle of the circle sat Nitis. He appeared to be deep in prayer. Kajika backed away so he didn't disturb Nitis's concentration.

"Come," Nitis said. "There's a pest I could use your help with. Given how many of my sprouts as he's eaten, the little devil must weigh as much as a buffalo. No matter what I do, he finds my plants. I've been trying to catch him for three seasons now."

As he followed, Kajika asked the question that he'd wondered about since he first heard about Nitis. "Do you not have family to provide for you?"

"The land provides all I need." He tipped his head in the direction of his cave. "But Ahyoka and Maska help to make my life easier."

"You're not related by blood?"

"No. At least not that I know of."

"I understood that you taught her mother?"

"Adsila was born with many natural abilities. She too could see and hear things that most men cannot. I only showed her how to use the gifts the land provides. Things like herbs. I also taught her the signs animals leave for us to mark the changing season or coming danger."

They walked for a while before Kajika also asked, "Why did you never take a wife and have a family of your own?"

"I did."

"What happened?"

"Like Adsila, my wife died trying to bring life into this world."

"I'm sorry."

"I made peace with my loss many seasons ago. I will see them both when my time comes to pass into the lands beyond."

"You seem certain of that."

Nitis stopped and turned to look at him. "I am."

Kajika took a step closer. "How?"

"Because of all that I have seen and heard in this lifetime." He gestured to the area around them. "Everything you see whispers its purpose, and if you listen close enough you can hear them say that even when their purpose is finished there is something more.

Something we'll find when only ash remains."

"Like what?"

"I believe that is different for everyone and everything." He leaned heavily upon his walking stick. "My question for you is do you know your purpose? In this life and in this place?"

Kajika contemplated the ground they stood upon before answering. "At one time I did. But now I'm not as certain."

"What changed?"

He looked in the direction of Nitis's cave. "Her."

"Why do you suppose that is?"

Kajika scrambled for an answer but couldn't find one. "I don't know."

"That's what scares you."

"Yes."

"Would it make you feel better if I told you your destinies were joined?"

Kajika frowned. "I'm not sure."

Nitis grunted. "Worry about it later. Right now, you have prey to catch." He pointed to a cluster of trees he had led them to. "The furry devil should be in there."

Kajika took a deep breath then nodded once. "I'll find him."

"I'll wait."

Silently Kajika crept into the brush.

Was it possible that he could have a life with Ahyoka? He'd grown to care for her. He wouldn't call it love, but he did worry for her well-being. Her beliefs were somewhat troubling, but who was he to say that she was wrong?

Chief Yonaguska respected her and, more importantly, Winema seemed to have genuine affection for her. Even the people of his village responded well to her while she visited. Perhaps his brother could give him advice about whether it would be a good alliance. He'd never had patience for the things that went on between tribes nor did he want to create a difficult situation for his chief.

The two women in his village he had considered taking as wife never pulled at him in the same way as Ahyoka. Would a marriage based solely on the need to fill a role be better than one of the heart? Dyami had taken a wife who had touched his heart. They had been a good match up until the end. Even Chief Yonaguska seemed to have chosen Winema for reasons other than an alliance. They cared deeply for each other.

Obviously love didn't turn those men into weak fools.

While thoughts churned in his mind, he allowed himself to get lost in the hunt. Not long after his frame of mind had returned to something normal, he rejoined Nitis and presented the results of his efforts.

"There were two of them?" Nitis exclaimed over the hares.

"You'll be lucky if there aren't more. Usually where there's a mated pair, there are more in the nest."

Nitis grumbled below his breath.

With a quick glance at the location of the sun, Kajika suggested, "If you're ready, we should return to the cave."

"Yes." Nitis slowly rose from the log he had been sitting on. "Perhaps Ahyoka will have prepared something for us to eat by now."

Kajika waited for Nitis to pass then followed him back to the cave.

Ahyoka greeted them at the entrance with a smile. "There you are."

The idea that she had been waiting for them to return, perhaps worrying about how they fared, felt right.

"I didn't know if you'd be back in time to cook whatever you caught, so I went ahead and started a stew from some of the things I gathered from your growing spot." She led the way inside. "It should be ready soon."

"How did you know he'd bring anything back?" Nitis asked.

She glanced over her shoulder and grinned. "Because he's a skilled hunter and he's proven his abilities every day I've travelled with him."

Kajika's chest puffed at her words.

She poured fresh water into bowls and handed one to both of them.

Nitis grunted then took his seat on the pile of furs near the fire.

"I'll start working on these." Kajika held up the hares he'd caught then asked Ahyoka, "Does he like them prepared in any special way?"

"No, not that he has ever mentioned." The corner of her lip lifted. "I think he's just grateful to not have to do it himself."

He nodded then stepped outside to take care of the messier part of meat preparation. Some shied away from this part of the hunt, finding it too gruesome, or perhaps just too messy, to be dealt with.

But he always found it soothing to go through the motions he'd learned from his father and grandfather.

No sooner had he hung the last skin for drying than Ahyoka joined him. "The stew is ready if you'd like to stop and eat."

"You have good timing." The meat still needed to be salted and the skins would need to be dried for several days, but Nitis could manage both of those things after they'd left.

"Nitis said he has something to share with us."

"Good news?"

"Hard to tell with Nitis. I'm guessing he learned something on his walk today." She held out a bucket. "I assume you want to clean up?"

"Definitely."

She poured water over his outstretched hands then handed him the bucket so he could finish. Once he felt clean, he rinsed his knives and returned them to his pouch. He took the linen she held in offering and dried his hands then his face.

The entire scene felt more domestic than he was used to. He'd witnessed similar behavior between couples he knew. It was a pleasant feeling. Having someone anticipate your needs and be willing to lend a hand whether you needed it or not.

Something else for him to consider.

He handed her back the linen. "I believe I'm ready to sample that stew you made."

She smiled. "Hopefully it will live up to your expectations. I'm no Winema when it comes to preparing food, but my brother and father have always liked my stew."

"I'm sure it will more than fill our bellies."

He placed his hand on her back and steered her toward the cave.

"Thank you."

"For what?" he asked.

"For catching and preparing the meat for Nitis. He does well enough on his own, but I can tell the years are catching up to him. I always worry he doesn't eat enough."

"I'm happy to help. If we had time, I'd catch more."

"I'm sure Maska will bring him a sizeable portion when they return from their hunt."

"Good."

When they stepped into the lit part of the cave, they found Nitis hobbling back to his pile of furs. It looked as if he had washed his face and hands. The fire light glinted off drops of water that clung to his strands of gray hair.

As gracefully as his aged body would let him, he lowered himself onto the furs. He set a jug next to his leg then motioned them forward. "The stew Ahyoka prepared for us is calling to me. Let us eat and I'll share what the ancients have whispered in my ear."

Once they had all settled around the fire and ate a few bites, Nitis began. "I told you last night that you needed to find this skinwalker and stop them."

Ahyoka and Kajika both nodded.

"What I didn't know then was why it was so important."

"You said the skinwalker would kill more people and gain more power," Ahyoka reminded him.

"That's true."

"So we just need to find him and stop him from killing anyone else," Kajika guessed.

Nitis's eyes turned a little hazy. "You won't have to look for the skinwalker. It will find you."

"Why is he so interested in us?" Ahyoka asked.

He leveled his gaze on her. "It's interested in you."

"Me?" She lowered the bowl she had been eating from.

Nitis nodded.

Kajika sat up at attention. His need to protect flared within his chest.

"Why me?" she asked.

"I suspect it has detected that not only do you walk with the spirits but that you also carry your father's warrior blood and your mother's healing abilities." He leveled a hard look upon her. "That would be an irresistible combination to someone seeking excessive power."

"Ghigau was supposed to be the daughter of a shaman," Kajika told him. "Is that why the skinwalker killed her?"

"Very likely." Nitis swung his gaze back to Ahyoka. "If it were to take your spirit energies, I'm not sure what it would do to them." Nitis tossed his stick into the fire. "But I would rather not find out."

"Agreed," Kajika said.

"What about Dyami and his wife and child? How do we free

them if—" She corrected herself. "When we are able to catch this skinwalker?"

"When were they killed?"

"Tonight will be the ninth passing of the moon. Brother Fox told me we had until the new moon to release their spirits. Otherwise they wouldn't be able to cross into the Great Hunting Grounds."

Nitis's frown deepened. "That's in two more nights."

"I know." Ahyoka's concern grew. "We need to find the killer soon. But what do we do once we find the skinwalker?"

"I believe the host can surrender what remains of the spirits they have taken," Nitis told them.

"How likely is that?" Kajika asked.

"Based on what you've told me and what the ancients are saying about this creature, I doubt they will do so willingly. I suspect there is little left of its humanity."

"What's the next option?" she asked.

"You may have no other choice but to kill the creature," Nitis told them. "When its own spirit energy is released, what is left of the others should be freed."

"But you aren't certain," Kajika said.

"I'm afraid not. I don't know of anyone who has dealt with this, so I'm basing my answer on what I know of spirits and what the ancients are telling me."

Kajika nodded in understanding.

"There's one other thing you should know," Nitis added.

"What's that?" Kajika asked with a touch of reluctance.

Nitis looked at each of them in turn. "The more fear its victims feel at death, the more power it absorbs."

"So if I have to die, don't be afraid?" Ahyoka asked.

"Yes," Nitis answered.

"How about if you just stay away from it and not die," Kajika told her.

"That would be a much better idea," Nitis said.

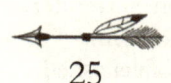

25

Ahyoka said her farewells to Nitis while Kajika readied the horses.

"Your destiny lies before you, child," Nitis told her as he watched Kajika. "It is time for Maska to take his place in the village."

"He will not like it."

"Maska will adapt." Nitis looked to Ahyoka. "Both men will." He put one hand on her shoulder. "Your children will be brave and strong. They will make fine warriors." His gaze drifted off and his eyes took on that white-ish glaze. "But your youngest will be the strongest of them all. She alone will be the window into the spirit world. And she will guard it fiercely. She will have to."

The fine hair on her arms stood on end. She looked to Kajika then pressed a hand to her belly. A vision of several dark-headed children playing in a field as she gathered herbs came to her. It filled her heart with joy and gave her hope that there might be more for them than this journey.

"Go. It is time," Nitis encouraged her.

She nodded mutely.

Kajika helped her climb onto her horse then went to his own mount. As they set off, she looked back at the cave entrance. Nitis watched them from his vantage point on the hill.

"What did Nitis say to you while I was preparing the horses?" Kajika asked.

She debated how much to tell him. "That Maska could no longer put off assuming his place as medicine man."

"Every village needs one."

She smiled. "Yes, but Maska doesn't understand why it must be him."

"Why does it have to be him?"

"Because it is his rightful place. He inherited the gifts. He simply chooses to ignore them."

"Why did you not step up and take the position?"

She looked him in the eye. "My destiny lies elsewhere."

He fell silent and returned to scanning the trees. They rode for some time without a word between them, each lost in their own thoughts. When they reached the shaded spot where they had stopped on their ride to Nitis's hill, they slowed and studied the area.

Something had disturbed the spirits.

Previously there had been a cool, welcoming feeling. Today, however, Ahyoka sensed something murky and sickly.

"Something is wrong," Kajika murmured.

She nodded.

"It's too quiet. The birds are not singing and the air feels stale." He moved his horse closer to hers.

"The creature has been here," she whispered.

"How long ago?"

"Less than a day." She met his gaze again. "Do you think he's going back to the village?"

"I don't know, but we should keep moving."

"What about the horses?"

"They will be fine for a while longer."

"And if we're forced to run?"

He grimaced. "They wouldn't make it far." He took a deep breath and looked about the area again. "A short rest. Stay near your horse."

She nodded and led her mount to a bush with berries it could eat. It must have sensed the same things as she and Kajika because it hesitated letting its guard down long enough to take refreshment. Only when she stroked its neck and murmured comforting words did it relent.

Kajika kept watch from a flat part of the bank. His bow lay across his lap with an arrow notched within the string. When her horse finished drinking from her hand, Kajika led his to her and handed her the reigns. "Can you hold them both while I keep watch?"

"Yes."

"If something happens, let mine loose. He won't go far without me."

"All right," she promised.

Kajika returned to his place along the edge of the clearing while the horses rested. As expected, he didn't allow them much time. They were remounted and moving on well before she even had a chance to look for the plants she often picked when she travelled this way.

Without being told, she remained silent until the sounds of woods and wind returned to its normal cadence.

The Spirit Talker comes!

Fair journey to you and yours.

"Why have you never taken a husband?"

Kajika's question startled her, not only due to its abruptness but also because of its deeply personal nature. "I, uh…" She played with her reigns. "Most of the men in my village keep their distance from me."

"Because of your father?"

"No. Because of my gifts. Many of the women do too. They appreciate my healings and most call for me when they're ill, but they've always treated me like a bit of an outsider. Never as one of them."

He frowned.

"After my mother died, no one understood that I could see and hear things they couldn't. Only Maska. Father knows I am not crazy, but since he doesn't have my gifts, he can't explain them. My aunt believes me when I tell her something, but she doesn't ask questions about how I know things."

"Do they treat Maska the same way?"

"No. He has always been better at hiding his abilities. For the longest time, I didn't realize he had any of Mother's gifts."

"You said he has been denying them."

"That's right."

"But he isn't now?"

She smiled. "Some gifts will not be denied no matter how much we fight them."

"I have a feeling you never fought yours."

Her heart warmed at the gentle understanding in his tone. "No,

I didn't. I did learn early on that I shouldn't flaunt my gifts. So if I can find a way to act on them without explaining, I do."

He fell silent for a moment again then asked, "Tell me something you can see or hear that I can't. At this moment."

She closed her eyes and listened to the voices around her. "There's a fox running to her den over there." She pointed off to his right.

"That could be written off as a good guess out here. What else?"

"Your horse didn't like the berries he found and ate last night. You should give him more water to flush them out and relieve the ache."

He glanced down. "He found berries he shouldn't have eaten?"

"I'm afraid so. He—"

Suddenly the voices around her cried out in alarm. There were so many so couldn't focus on any one of them to know where the danger came from. From the corner of her eye she saw a dark beast charging out of the bushes in their direction. Kajika's horse reared back in alarm and tossed him to one side.

Ahyoka's horse also jumped, forcing her to wrestle with control of her mount and stay on her seat.

"Go!" Kajika roared.

She kneed her horse and urged it into a run to get away. But when she glanced over her shoulder to see if the beast followed, she saw Kajika being knocked to the ground.

She pulled up on her reins and turned her horse around.

Kajika had rolled to the side. He leapt to his feet and pulled his knife from his belt. His bow and arrow lay somewhere off to the side, probably where they had been knocked out of his hands. Bloody gashes crossed one of his arms, yet he faced the beast without flinching.

The beast's movements were choppy and irregular. As if it struggled to control every action. She still didn't know exactly what they were confronting. Its size and shape were unlike anything she had ever seen before.

Then the putrid scent of rotting flesh hit her.

This had to be the skinwalker.

She swung her leg over the horse and leapt to the ground. She let the reins drop loose for fear that tethering him would make him more vulnerable if attacked. As soon as she stepped away, she called up on the spirits to reveal what they were dealing with.

The familiar warmth of energy rippled across her skin. The voices rushed into her head, calling out warnings and urging her to leave.

The beast's head whipped around. The cold, dead eyes landed on her as if it had scented new prey.

Kajika used the distraction to leap at the beast. His knife arced over and downward, but the beast jumped aside, causing his blow to miss its mark. With a snarl, the beast crawled back into the nearby bushes.

Was it hiding, waiting for another chance to strike?

"Are you all right?" she called out.

Without taking his eyes off the bushes, he yelled back, "Yes."

She jogged closer. "It's the skinwalker."

"That's what I guessed. Didn't look like a normal wolf and it smelled like that thing we ran into a couple days ago."

"Like death."

He nodded then took a couple of steps toward his bow and arrow. When he reached for them, the beast charged again. It hit Kajika in the side before he could get the arrow. The two of them rolled and tumbled until he managed to kick the beast off of him.

Ahyoka dug in her bag for her herbs while keeping one eye on the fight. If she could strip the skinwalker of its animal form, Kajika would have a much better chance of beating it.

She found three of the herbs she needed, but the fourth eluded her. She specifically remembered adding it before she left home, so she knew it had to be in there. Finally she found it.

She stripped the leaves from the stems then rolled the dried herbs together between her hands as she murmured a fervent prayer. When she felt they were mixed together, she darted as close to the fight as she dared.

With one last prayer to the spirits for their guidance, she tossed the herbal mixture into the air and blew it in the direction of the beast. The wind picked up the flakes and leaves and twisted them all over the beast.

It threw back its head with a howl and backed away. It shook its head several times, as if to clear the tiny pieces, but the wind kept up its barrage.

Bit by bit the black fur and flesh fell from the beast's body, leaving only the head of the previously slain wolf and their attacker.

Ahyoka's mouth fell open in surprise.

"A woman is behind everything?" Kajika asked.

The beast launched herself at Kajika. In his shock, he didn't prepare himself for the blow. His head snapped back and he stumbled backward. His foot caught on an exposed root and he hit the ground.

A dull thud told Ahyoka that Kajika had hit something hard when he fell. The way his eyes rolled back in his head confirmed it. Instead of springing back to his feet, he lay motionless.

"Kajika!"

The beast-woman's attention leapt her way.

Nitis's warnings echoed in her head. She couldn't let her spirit energies be taken. If she did, the creature would take Kajika's too and then they would all be lost.

26

She had to distract the beast-woman away from Kajika. Her heart hurt knowing he was vulnerable. There would be little Ahyoka could do to the beast-woman physically based on how strong her attacker appeared, but she couldn't stand by and do nothing.

"Who are you?" Ahyoka asked.

"Why does that matter to you?" The beast-woman's voice crackled, as if she hadn't used it in a while.

"Because I'd like to understand." She took a few steps to her right, hoping it would keep the beast-woman's attention on her instead of Kajika.

"Understand what?"

"Did you enter my father's tepee? Uninvited?"

The woman shook off the last of the fur and skin she wore. "I may have. I visit a lot of tepees while people are away." Her matted, dirty hair hung limply down her back. The patches of dirt on the knees of her buckskin pants made it look as if she crawled as much as she walked.

"Why?"

"It's how I survive. People never miss a strip or two of meat. Or an egg here or there." Her face twisted into a snarl. "I don't have someone to hunt for me. I do what I can to help myself."

Ahyoka took a couple more steps, putting Kajika behind the beast-woman. "I meant why did you choose my father's tepee instead of one of the others in the village?"

For a moment the woman's eyes rolled about, unfocused.

"Because I needed to."

"Why did you take the bracelet?"

"I needed it."

"Why?"

"Why are you asking me so many questions?" the beast-woman demanded.

"I told you. I want to understand."

"It will not help you."

"Why did you kill the man in the village to the west?" Ahyoka changed topics, hoping to throw her off.

"I needed the woman. He was in my way."

"Why did you need the woman?"

"Because she had power."

Ahyoka blinked. "What power?"

"Power like yours."

"I have no power."

"Yes, you do. I feel it." The beast-woman took a step toward Ahyoka. "Even now. Even though you aren't drawing on it. I felt it earlier."

"I don't know what you mean," Ahyoka lied and took a step back. "What about the woman you killed?"

"I'd been trying to find her for some time. I knew that she'd gone to Yonaguska's village, but it took a while to figure out which one she was." She grinned in an eerie way. "Crafty that one. Always with the other women. Made it hard to tell who had the power."

"What power?"

The woman wagged a finger at her. "No use trying to fool me. I know you have it too. You may not be one of them, but I can't pass up the gift the Great Spirit has presented me with."

"One of who?"

The woman's face darkened. "Them. All of them. The men who turned me out. Said I abused my position and had tried to seduce that stinking man on the tribal council. They wouldn't listen. They didn't believe that it was him."

A horrible picture began to solidify in Ahyoka's mind. A picture describing what this woman tried not to say. "What did he do?"

"What didn't he do? Always touching where he shouldn't. Trying to bribe his way out of trouble. Never satisfied." The beast-woman's eyes turned a light shade of yellow. "Never accepting when someone told him no."

"And he got away with it, didn't he?"

"Yes!" The beast-woman's voice echoed and carried a hint of some kind of magic. "But no longer." She stomped toward Ahyoka with a determined look on her face. "If they won't listen to me, then I will stop him myself. For good."

Ahyoka backed up a few steps. "How do you plan to do that?"

"Once I take your power, I will have enough that they won't be able to stop me. Not even their so-called medicine man."

"I'm not sure you know what you're doing or what you think you need."

"Yes I do. I've never been more sure. I will end his abuse and I will make sure they pay. All of them."

As the beast-woman leapt, she pulled a knife from some hidden pocket and aimed it at Ahyoka. Ahyoka grabbed the woman's wrist and fought to keep the blade away. They twisted and turned in a grotesque dance until the beast-woman backed Ahyoka into a tree.

Ahyoka sent out a distress call to the spirits around them, asking for help and their protection.

"I knew it!" the woman screeched. "You do have power." She grabbed Ahyoka by the throat and slammed her against the tree.

Ahyoka grunted from the blow and swallowed the ache that rippled through her chest. When the beast-woman raised the knife again, Ahyoka lifted her foot, wedged it between them, and pushed the woman back. She spun away from the tree and tried to put a little more distance between them. The beast-woman pounced on her, sending them both to the ground.

Keeping one eye on the knife, Ahyoka fought with everything she had, but the beast-woman outmatched her in strength. Before she knew it, Ahyoka found herself on her back pinned beneath the woman. Ahyoka clawed at the beast-woman's hand, but the woman's filthy digits only tightened around her neck.

Ahyoka's heart pounded in her chest. She needed more air, but she couldn't let go of her grip on the woman's knife hand. Tiny spots began to dance in the corner of her vision. With a cry, the woman pulled the knife back.

A thud sounded and the beast-woman's body jerked. She froze and her eyes widened in fear. Her grip on Ahyoka's neck loosed. Ahyoka sucked in a much needed lungful of air. Another thud sounded and the knife slipped from the woman's hand. The beast-woman turned and tipped to one side, off of Ahyoka.

Ahyoka rolled away from the woman, coughing from the rush of air.

With a shriek, the woman reached over her shoulder and ripped one of the arrows out. She spun around and rushed toward Kajika.

She'd only taken a few steps when a bobcat raced out of the brush and into the side of her leg. The beast-woman tripped and fell to the ground. Before she could get back onto her feet, a warning growl came from another bush. A sleek, silver and black wolf stepped into view. Its teeth were bared and its eyes focused solely on the beast-woman.

"Go!" the beast-woman shouted at the wolf, but the massive creature ignored her command and advanced on her.

Kajika and Ahyoka froze in place. Ahyoka held her breath and waited. Her call for help had been answered.

The bobcat flattened its ears and moved toward the beast-woman from his side of the area.

The beast-woman looked from one creature to the other, shaking the bloody arrow at both. "Get away from me!" Even though she used her power to command them, they didn't stop.

Tree limbs crackled from somewhere behind the beast-woman, drawing everyone's attention. One of the largest brown bears Ahyoka had ever seen burst from the foliage and charged the beast-woman. The beast-woman's eyes widened in alarm, but she held her ground. She turned the arrow on the bear. "Stop!"

Ahyoka sensed power behind the woman's words, but it had no effect on any of the animals.

The bear barreled into the beast-woman, knocking her to the ground. Then with one mighty swipe of his paw, bone crunched and blood arced into the air. The massive creature then stood on its back legs and let out a roar. The sound echoed through the area and made Ahyoka flinch with its finality.

It is done.

After giving the beast-woman one last sniff, the bear ambled back into the woods the way it had come. The wolf held Ahyoka's gaze for a moment. *Go in peace, Spirit Talker.* Then it too, turned and disappeared behind the trees.

The bobcat's tail twitched. *See to your mate, sister. And have a care for yourself also.* With those last instructions, it took off in a different direction than the other two.

"Are you all right?" Kajika asked.

She nodded and took his hand. "What about you?"

"Other than a headache, yes." He looked at the brush where the bear and wolf had gone. "That was… unusual."

"I agree."

Kajika's expression darkened. He gestured to where the beast-woman had fallen. "We should make sure she's not a threat."

With a grimace, Ahyoka said, "I don't know how she could be now."

"I don't either, but I'm not about to chance it." He guided her to where the beast-woman lay on the ground. The ground next to her had darkened with blood. There were four deep gouges across the woman's chest and neck. Her eyes were open and she gasped for air.

The woman locked gazes with Ahyoka and rasped between breaths, "You let them win."

"No, I didn't. Your hatred of them turned you into a monster. That's not justice."

"It certainly wasn't justice when you killed my cousin, his wife, and their child," Kajika added.

"I did—" She gasped for air. "—what I had to do."

"The path you followed could only lead to death," Ahyoka pointed out. "The Great Spirit will decide your fate now. The least you could do is release the souls that you have taken without mercy."

"No." She shook her head, making the blood at her neck flow more. "I need…" The beast-woman's eyes widened as if she saw something terrifying standing behind them.

The hair on Ahyoka's neck stood on end. She slipped her hand into Kajika's and whispered, "Go gather wood for a fire. Quickly. We need to release Dyami and the others. Since she will not willingly give them up, we need to burn the body as soon as she takes her last breath. It won't be long now."

He nodded and headed to the treed area just to their right. As soon as he turned his back to her, she let out the breath she had been holding and swiveled to see what waited behind her.

The hazy figure of an ancient warrior sitting upon a magnificent horse stood not far away watching the beast-woman.

Waiting.

Waiting to take her spirit to the land beyond. On the journey where she would be judged.

If the look on her face had been any sign, Ahyoka guessed even the beast-woman didn't like what her fate might be.

27

Kajika placed the final log next to the beast-woman's body. She'd known what they planned to do even as she drew her last breath. He'd allowed himself a brief moment of guilt over the fact that he'd been relieved when her body went lax and her raspy breathing ceased.

Now he needed to do whatever he had to in order to save Dyami and Dyami's family. Even if it meant setting aside all of his doubts about spirits and talking animals.

"Here." Ahyoka handed him the stones he needed to spark a flame to life.

She appeared to be holding herself together despite the day's events. He wondered why she kept glancing to the east. As far as he could tell, nothing was there. He hated to guess what she might see though.

He rearranged a couple of smaller sticks that had been partially covered by dried leaves and grass. "Ready?"

She nodded once.

With practiced ease, he lit the dried pieces, then worked the small flame into a larger one until the larger branches began to catch fire.

Ahyoka made a circuit around the fire, chanting prayers for the dead and their passing. He wondered if they were meant for the beast-woman or for those she'd killed. Occasionally she tossed herbs onto the pyre. Each time she did, the flame reached higher and took on a different color—colors he'd never seen in a normal fire.

Finally the fire grew large enough that he felt certain it had reached the beast-woman's body. The smoke turned dark and grew thick and choking.

Ahyoka's chants grew in volume and intensity. Part of him wished he knew the ritual so he could aid her. But something in his gut told him to simply keep watch and ensure her safety.

Just when he thought he would have to pull her away from the black haze, the wind swirled into the clearing and broke through the cloud of smoke. Within the wind he thought he heard the pounding of a horse's hooves. Once the wind passed, the smoke lightened and transformed into what he expected to see with a normal fire.

Ahyoka stumbled and swayed on her feet. He rushed to her side, catching her before she hit the ground.

"What's wrong?" He wiped the beads of sweat from her forehead.

"I'm sorry. Her spirit put up quite the fight. The horseman had to intervene."

The hair on the back of his neck stood on end. "The horseman?"

She nodded and tried to get up, but he held her in his lap.

"Her final ride. Where she will be judged."

"So it's true then."

"Oh, yes, most definitely."

"What about Dyami? Did the horseman take him? And Ghigau and the baby?"

She frowned. "No, I don't think so, but I lost focus when they rode past me."

They both looked at the fire.

In disbelief, Kajika watched as the hazy image of his cousin stepped out of the fire and came to stand before them.

Ahyoka bowed her head respectfully, but Kajika was too stunned to move.

"Cousin." Dyami's voice sounded as if it echoed through a deep valley.

"Are you real?" Kajika reached for his cousin.

Ahyoka grabbed his hand to stop him. She mumbled something about it being disrespectful, but her words didn't register with him. The shock at seeing Dyami in this state overrode all thoughts.

Dyami smiled sadly. "Do not be afraid, cousin. I'm more of a memory to you than anything else. I only wanted to thank you for finding and freeing us." He looked back at the burning debris. "An eternity without Ghigau is unthinkable."

"So you're both free then?" Kajika asked.

"Yes." He held his hand out to the fire. The nearly transparent figure of Ghigau stepped out, carrying their child, and took Dyami's hand. "Thanks to the two of you."

"I'm glad we were able to find you in time," Ahyoka told them.

"So are we." Dyami and Ghigau looked to the west then Dyami nodded his head once, as if answering a summons. "But now we must go."

"Peace be with you in the Great Hunting Grounds," Ahyoka said.

"And to you, Spirit Talker," Dyami said.

Kajika finally shook off his stupor. "Save a few buffalo for me. I'll come find you when it's my time."

Dyami smiled. "I will. But you have many seasons before then."

As they walked away, Dyami turned and yelled over his shoulder, "Be patient with him, Spirit Talker. He will make a fine husband and give you many strong children. Just don't expect him to know how to clean an infant."

Kajika smiled at the memory as he and Ahyoka watched the hazy figures disappear into the sunset.

After the sun tipped over the horizon, Ahyoka stirred. "Are you all right?"

He took a deep breath. "Yes." He looked down at her and marveled at all that this tiny woman could do. How she could be so strong and so vulnerable at the same time.

"I'm glad we were able to free Dyami, Ghigau, and the baby so they can be together now."

"I am too." He frowned. "How was I able to see them though?"

She sat up. "I, uh…" She bit one side of her lip.

"You can tell me. I'm not angry. Just curious."

"I'm not completely sure. I suspect a lot of it was as Dyami said, that you were seeing more memory than spirit. But…"

He waited for her to continue.

"It may have been because you held me across your lap."

He frowned. "You think my touching you somehow allowed

me to see them?"

"Maybe. You felt the flow of energy that time you held me, when you insisted I didn't walk on my injured foot."

"True." He climbed to his feet then reached for her hand to help her stand. "Do you think it's possible that the Great Spirit knew I needed to see Dyami one last time? So I could see that he and Ghigau made it safely to the Great Hunting Grounds?"

"Yes. I do think that is possible."

He nodded once, satisfied the matter had been settled. "Do you want to make camp here? Or put out the fire and resume our trek to your village?"

She crinkled her nose. "I don't think I'd be able to sleep if we stayed here. Too much went on here."

"I agree." He glanced about the clearing. "It's too bad we don't have a jug to carry water."

"I think it burned hot enough that most of the wood is gone now." She lifted her nose into the air and sniffed. "The coals may simmer for a day or two, but the coming rain will take care of what's left."

"It's going to rain?"

"Yes. And soon too."

He shook his head. "I'm not even going to ask how you know that."

She grinned and pointed to the south. "The dark raincloud heading this way is how I know."

"Are we going to get rained on if we keep riding?"

"Very likely."

He shrugged and went in search of his bow and arrows. "A little rain never hurt anyone."

After finding and coaxing both of their horses back, he checked their reins and strappings to make sure nothing had come loose. Ahyoka had sprinkled more herbs about the area and now appeared to be in search of plants.

"Are you ready to ride?" he asked after securing his bow.

"Yes. I just need to put these in my satchel." She held up a handful of plants.

He chuckled to himself. She needed a tepee just for drying her herbs. He led her horse to her then helped her climb up onto its back. While she settled herself, he mounted his own.

"You know we won't be able to make it to your village before dark," he pointed out as they urged the horses forward.

"Yes, I know." She glanced back at the still smoldering fire. "But I'm sure we can find a place to stop for the night."

He grunted in agreement.

They rode in silence until they reached the plain where they turned south.

"You've handled this ordeal well for someone who doesn't believe in spirits and things he cannot see or touch."

"But I did see Dyami." He furrowed his brow. "At least I think I did."

"We both saw him," she said. "And Ghigau."

He nodded. "Chief Yonaguska will be pleased to know we found the killer."

"What will you tell him?"

"That we found the killer and they have been dealt with."

"As little as possible then?"

"Something like that."

"I doubt Winema will be satisfied with that answer."

"Probably not." He shrugged. "If she presses, I'll tell her the truth. But I'd rather not tell the elders everything." He looked at her. "I've learned that not everyone is understanding about things beyond our normal day and night."

"That is very true."

"You've lived with that your whole life, haven't you?"

She turned her face away from him, but not before he saw the sadness that touched her expression. "I wasn't always aware of it."

"That doesn't make it fair."

"No. But no one ever said the path we were meant to follow would be easy to travel."

"No. They also didn't say you had to travel it alone."

28

Ahyoka's heart skipped a beat.

Before she could contemplate what he meant by his remark, a man yelled across the plain. "It's a little late for travel."

Kajika move his horse closer to hers and loosened the strap securing his bow.

Her head whipped in the direction of the voice. "Father! Maska!" She nudged her horse forward. "How was the hunt?"

"Good," her father, Paco, responded.

Neither of them said anything else until they drew closer.

"Imagine our disappointment to learn that, instead of a night of rest inside my tepee, we needed to rush after you."

"And your escort," Maska added.

She gestured to Kajika. "Father, Kajika is Chief Yonaguska's most honored warrior. He offered his protection while you and Maska were away."

"I'd like to know what she needed protection from," Maska pointed out.

"That is a long story," Kajika told them. "Would you prefer to have this conversation now or after stopping for the night?"

"That might be best," Paco answered. "There is a place not far from here that would be good."

Kajika tipped his head then he and Maska fell in behind Paco and Ahyoka.

Ahyoka quizzed them about their hunt along the way. As promised, it didn't take them long to reach the place her father had

155

mentioned.

Kajika and Maska tended to the horses while Paco pulled Ahyoka aside.

"You are well, daughter?" Paco touched the cut on her cheek.

"I am." She glanced in Kajika's direction. "We both are."

"Based on the little bit we were told by Hiamovi, I suspect you have an interesting story to tell."

"The last few days have been—" She grimaced. "—an adventure."

Paco chuckled. "I hate to point it out, but your mother and I met because of an adventure."

"I thought you met at a tribal council gathering."

"We did."

"So there was more to the story than just her helping with your injury then?"

His eyes took on the faraway look that he always got when he talked about her mother.

"Who had an injury?" Maska asked when he and Kajika joined them.

"No one. Father was just talking about one of his former hunts."

"I assume you two brought food with you?" She gestured at Kajika. "We only packed enough for the day, and I'm guessing no one wants to go to the trouble of hunting something and cooking it?"

"We brought plenty for all of us," Paco motioned to the satchel that Maska carried.

She portioned out food for everyone while Maska gathered sticks and smaller pieces of wood for a fire. Paco quizzed Kajika about his people and his recent hunt. By the time she and Maska had finished their chores, she felt certain Kajika and her father had reached some accord and were getting along.

Based on the glances Maska kept shooting at Kajika, she wasn't sure he had gotten comfortable yet. Why it mattered to her so much, she couldn't say. After all, she shouldn't think more of Kajika than any other guest. He would be leaving tomorrow, and the odds of seeing him again were small unless she were to visit Winema.

With that depressing thought weighing on her heart, she took her seat next to her father. Once Maska sat down, Paco asked,

"Start at the beginning. I understand Ahyoka found her way to your village and then you both travelled to ours."

"That's partially correct."

Ahyoka remained silent while Kajika told them everything that had happened. He included everything from the time he learned of Dyami's death. Obviously he realized there would be little point hiding anything. Her father and Maska were both familiar with her gifts and never batted an eye.

Occasionally one of them asked for clarification. And a few times Maska asked her what she had seen or which herbs she used. By the time Kajika finished relaying the events and answering their questions, the day's events had caught up to her. Her eyes became heavy not long after eating.

Without realizing he had even gotten up and retrieved it, Kajika handed her the blanket she traveled with. "Go ahead and get some sleep. I'll stay up with your father. You're well protected tonight."

Paco nodded in agreement. "Sleep, daughter. You've had a tiresome day."

Unable to do otherwise, she did as they suggested and lay down with her head on her satchel and the blanket wrapped around her shoulders. Her dreams were busy and colorful. Voices flitted in and out of her consciousness, but none of them left a clear impression.

She slowly came awake to the soft light filtering through the trees. She rolled over and looked around the circle their group had formed. As expected, she found Kajika's spot empty. She listened, hoping he may have gotten up to relieve himself, but she knew in her heart he had left to return to his own village.

It would have been further for him to travel if he went with them before travelling home. And he would have had a hard time refusing the gifts her father would have forced upon him as thanks for his protection. But she would have liked to have told him good-bye.

Her foolish heart told her that she would see him again, even as it wept the loss.

She soothed herself by connecting with the land. The voices that were always around her came into focus.

The rain.
The rain.
It comes.

She had thought the route her father had taken would keep

them out of the rain. But a gentle shower would be welcomed to wash some of the smoke and dust from her face and hair. When they made it home, she would take a cleansing bath in the river. She needed to feel the healing waters across her skin almost as much as she needed a few nights on her own sleeping mat.

The pitter-patter of the rain on the canopy of leaves above her lulled her back into a light sleep. As she dozed, she dreamed.

In her dream, she saw the silhouette of a woman dressed in pristine white skins walking toward her through a long passage of arching trees. Ahyoka sat up from where she had been lying on the ground when the woman drew close. The woman knelt in front of her, bringing her face into focus.

In a breathless whisper, Ahyoka acknowledged the woman. "Mother."

Her mother reached out and caressed her cheek, but Ahyoka could only feel a cool brush of air.

"How are you here?" Ahyoka asked.

"The Great Spirit allowed me to seek you out to tell you that you did well by stopping Hania."

"Who?"

"The one you called beast-woman. By dealing with her fairly and trusting in your calling, you stopped her from killing any more innocents, yet saved yourself and your future from the taint of her hatred and darkness. Had you spilled her blood yourself, you would have never been free of the stain. The Great Spirit is pleased."

"Thank you."

"I've been instructed to tell you that because of your faithfulness to the old ways, you will receive new blessings in the days to come."

Ahyoka's eyes widened and her heart kicked up a beat.

"You must prepare yourself for the next part of your journey. Heal your body, calm your mind, and soothe your heart." Her mother smiled. "And know that you are loved."

Ahyoka tried to grasp her mother's hand, but her own passed right through. "What if I cannot do what the Great Spirit needs?"

"I believe you can." Her mother rose to her feet. "Besides, no one said you would walk your path alone."

"What about the ones Hania believed to have wronged her?"

Her mother's lips pinched into a grim line. "Their punishments have been decided. It is not for you to worry with." She took a step back. "I must go. I was only granted a few moments with you."

"I miss you," Ahyoka told her.

"I've missed you also. But you know I've never been far."

Ahyoka sniffled and nodded.

"Be happy, my little bird." Her mother turned to walk back down the path she'd come. Then over her shoulder, she added, "And tell your brother that destiny waits for no one."

"Any message for Father?" she shouted to her mother's back.

"Your father knows everything that is in my heart."

With tears in her eyes, she watched until her mother disappeared at the end of the trail. With a blink, she awoke in her place next to the now banked fire. Her father sat nearby eating a piece of dried meat and watching her.

"You saw your mother, didn't you?" he asked.

Ahyoka sat up. "Yes." She pulled her blanket tightly about her shoulders. "How did you know?"

He rolled the piece he had been eating between his thumb and finger. "You spoke her name."

"Did I say anything else?"

"No, why?"

"She gave me a message for Maska."

His brow lifted. "But not one for me?"

She shook her head. "She said you know everything that is in her heart."

He gave her a sad smile. "I guess I do." He finished the last bites of meat then offered her a couple of pieces from his satchel.

Even though she didn't have much of an appetite, she took them.

"The rain has mostly passed. We should start making our way home," he told her.

She nodded.

"Your brother is tending to the horses." He climbed to his feet then reached to help her up.

"I only need a moment to be ready."

Without releasing her, he asked, "You haven't asked about Kajika."

"I'm guessing he left before daybreak to go back to his village."

Paco gave her a brisk nod.

"He has been gone from his village for many days. I'm sure Yonaguska and his people need him."

"Yes," he murmured. "I'm sure they do."

"And Yonaguska needs to be told the danger is gone and that Dyami has been avenged."

"His people need the closure." With one finger, he lifted her chin until she met his gaze. "But what do you need, daughter?"

"To rest and then wait to see what the Great Spirit has in store for me."

He held her gaze, as if searching for an answer. Finally, he nodded, satisfied by whatever he found. "Let's go home. I believe we're all overdue for some rest."

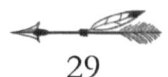

29

Kajika led the way into Ahyoka's village. More than one person stopped and stared before hurrying on, probably to tell someone else what they'd seen. It wouldn't take long for word to reach the elders of their arrival.

Sure enough, before they'd passed two more tepees, one of the elders he'd seen on his previous visit came out to greet them.

"Where can we find Chief Hiamovi?" Kajika asked the elder.

"He's looking over the new structure our men are building." He gestured toward the far end of the village. "You can come with me to the gathering place. I'll have one of the boys let him know you have returned."

Kajika nodded. When he was satisfied the elder had done as he promised, he nudged his horse forward.

"Are we dressed strange? Or do they not get many guests?" Even though Winema's question had been asked in a low tone, Kajika had still been able to pick up on it.

"I'm not sure. Most people do seem to be astounded seeing us here," Chief Yonaguska whispered back.

"I suspect many of their visitors are traders or relatives from other villages. I doubt any other chiefs have come by unexpectedly," Kajika said over his shoulder.

The elder stumbled to a halt. "Did you say chief?"

"Yes," Kajika told him.

The elder's eyes widened and darted toward Yonaguska and Winema. He gestured for two of the women lingering nearby to come forward. "Run ahead and tell Dichali the chief has honored guests and to prepare refreshments for them."

Kajika exchanged glances with Yonaguska. In their village, it didn't matter who had come to visit. All guests were honored.

The elder gestured for them to continue. "The gathering place is this way."

They rode the rest of the way in silence. Thankfully, Chief Yonaguska and Winema would provide enough of a distraction that he wouldn't have to interact with Chief Hiamovi. His nerves were already on edge. He doubted he'd be able to take much of the pompous and arrogant attitude Hiamovi had displayed last time he'd been here.

He had come to see Ahyoka.

When they reached the gathering place, a couple of younger men came forward to help with their horses. Then two women brought jugs of water and folded linens for them to wash their face and hands. By the time they had relieved their thirst, Chief Hiamovi arrived along with the small party of elders that seemed to follow him on official business.

The two chiefs greeted each other formally. Yonaguska had explained on their ride that he did indeed know Hiamovi but not very well. He thought it possible they were related through his father's family but couldn't remember where that connection had been.

As they talked, Kajika scanned the faces of those lingering outside of the gathering place. He knew instinctively the one he searched for would not be there. He would have known if she were.

Finally he did see Paco striding toward them. The short amount of time he'd spent with Paco on the trip back from Nitis's had left him with the impression that Ahyoka's father was a quietly proud man. A skilled warrior, yet not boastful. Much like Kajika's own father.

He rose to greet Paco at the edge of their rapidly growing crowd.

"Kajika, it is good to see you again. I trust your journey home went well?"

"It did. I made good time. Yonaguska was relieved to learn we had found the person responsible for my cousin's death. And to know that there would be no further attacks."

"I'm sure he was." He glanced toward the two chiefs. "You did not travel alone?"

"No. Yonaguska said it had been many seasons since he had visited with Chief Hiamovi and wanted to renew that friendship." He tipped his head to one side. "Maska did not come with you?"

"He and I were working on a hide. He will come as soon as he cleans up." Paco grinned. "Is Maska the only one of my children you are concerned about?"

"No, but I didn't expect Ahyoka to come to the gathering no matter who the visitors were." He frowned. "Is she well? Did her foot finish healing?"

"Yes. It took her a few days to recover from your travels, but I haven't noticed a limp or any sign that her foot bothers her at all."

"Good. I feared that not being off of it after her injury would slow its healing."

"She has been unusually quiet though. And she spends a great deal of time near the river." He clasped Kajika's shoulder. "If you grow weary of this conversation—" He tipped his head toward the group hovering around the two chiefs. "—you will most likely find her there."

"Thank you. To be honest, I was ready to get away from this crowd as soon as we arrived."

Paco chuckled. "Why do you think I took my time coming?"

The two of them rejoined the group. Kajika made the introductions to Yonaguska and Winema.

"You're Ahyoka's father?" Winema asked. "I'm disappointed she didn't come with you. Is she at home?"

"She is most likely gathering herbs," Paco told them.

"Kajika, you know your way about here, do you not?" Winema asked. "Why don't you go and find her. I would love to see her again."

Kajika stifled his grin at her matchmaking attempts. "I will do what I can to find her."

Winema waved him on. "I have faith in you. You can track anything."

Paco gave him a quick nod over Winema's head. Without excusing himself from either of the chiefs, he slipped through the crowd and headed toward the river.

Not wanting to draw any more attention than necessary, he kept his pace brisk but not at a run. As he drew near the place he expected to find her, he slowed his pace. He listened to the sounds and checked for unusual scents. It occurred to him that the things he did instinctively when he hunted were not all that different than when she used her gifts.

The Great Spirit provided scents, sounds, colors, and other clues. Perhaps it was simply how people interpreted those things. Not everyone looked for those things or bothered to learn about the world around them. Now that Ahyoka had opened his eyes to her world, he found it easier to find the answers he needed when he relaxed and took it all in.

He followed the direction his gut told him to take, and soon he found what he'd been searching for. Ahyoka stood next to the river looking down into the water.

From the shadows of the tree behind her, he allowed himself a moment to admire her figure. He frowned. She looked thinner than when he'd last seen her. Had she been ill? Her father hadn't mentioned it.

She could have been on death's doorstep and she would still be beautiful. His blood stirred and his body warmed as he recalled the way he had brought her to pleasure not far from this very spot.

She turned and looked at him.

He stepped out of the shadows. "You don't seem surprised to see me."

She gestured to the trees. "They told me you had come."

He moved closer. "Makes it hard to sneak up on you."

Her lips twitched. "Maska always hated it."

"I'm sure he did." He ran his fingers along the braid she had woven in one side of her hair. "Have you been well?"

A tremor ran through her. "I… Yes." She took a step back. "What about you?"

"Yes." He clenched his fist at his side to keep from reaching for her. "I will admit to sleeping for the better part of a day after I returned home."

She nodded. "You went through a lot in a short span of time. I'm sure you were exhausted."

"We both went through a lot." He glanced down at her feet. "Your father said your foot had healed and that it didn't seem to give you any problems."

She lifted her foot and flexed it in a circle. "It did heal. I don't even notice it anymore."

"Good. I came back to—"

"You saw father?"

"Yes. I saw him at the gathering place. I introduced him to Yonaguska and Winema."

Her eyes widened. "Winema and the chief are here?"

He nodded. "Yonaguska wanted to renew the alliance with your people."

"Oh." She turned and faced the river once again. Disappointment rolled off her.

"I would think that you would agree with an alliance between our people."

She glanced his way. "Oh, I do."

He moved closer. "Then why do you look sad?"

"I had thought..." She bit her lip.

"What did you think?"

"Just a strange notion. It doesn't matter." Her smile appeared forced. "Are there many gathered for your visit?"

"More than my last visit."

She started forward then grimaced. "I doubt I'll be able to bring Winema back to our tepee to visit."

"Unlikely. And I doubt Yonaguska will let her leave him alone with Chief Hiamovi."

She shook her head. "I don't blame him."

When she started forward, he caught her by the arm. "I wanted to talk with you before you went to the gathering place."

"What about?"

"About you and I."

She blinked up at him. A knot curled in his gut. Why did the thought of asking her if she would take him as a husband make him sweat? He was a warrior. He had stared down angry bears and hungry wolves without losing his calm, but this tiny woman stirred far more emotions in him than he'd ever known existed.

"What about us?" she prompted.

"I, uh..." He slid his hand down her arm to her wrist. "We spent a lot of time together and it—"

She took a step back, breaking contact with him. "If you're worried that you have some obligation to me just because no one from my family travelled with us, you can stop. Father believes you to be an honorable man and will not force you into anything."

"No, I don't believe that he would. What I meant to say wa—"

"And I certainly didn't say anything to anyone about..." Her cheeks turned pink.

"I didn't think you had. I just wanted to—"

"Winema didn't say anything to you, did she? She's a bit of a matchmaker, you know."

"No, she didn't—"

"Good. She's my friend, but—"

"Can I just ask you something?"

She blinked at his outburst. "Go ahead."

"Have you ever thought about living somewhere other than here?"

"I..." She pushed a pebble around with her toe. "Yes, I have. Why?"

"I've been thinking about the time we spent together and how well we got along."

"Yes." She nodded. "We did seem to work well together."

"It has been brought to my attention that I have reached an age where I should consider taking a wife. After our adventure, I wondered how well we might do together." Despite his efforts to remain calm, his heart hammered in his chest.

"Are you asking me if I would take you as husband?"

"Yes." He held his breath even as his heart pounded in his chest. When did her answer become so important to him?

"Why?"

He frowned. "Why?"

"Yes." She stepped closer. "Why?"

"I told you. Based on how well we got along during our search for Dyami's killer, I think it likely we would do well together on a normal basis. Don't you?"

"Yes, I do."

"So you agree then?"

"I agree, but I didn't say I would take you as husband."

"Why not?"

"You haven't given me enough reason to do so."

"Are you worried I cannot provide for you?"

"No."

"Do you think I wouldn't make a good husband?"

"No, I think you are a good hunter and will be able to provide for a wife and family. You're a respected warrior. Your village values your contribution and they listen when you offer opinions or suggestions. My entire village thinks of me as the slightly crazy daughter of their best warrior. If not for him, I would have probably been driven out long ago. I don't want to diminish your standing with your people."

"From what I can see, your chief has set the tone for how your people treat you." He ground his teeth. "I don't agree with it. And I most certainly don't like it."

"Thank you." She took a deep breath. "My other hesitation lies in how you feel about me." She held up one finger to stop him when he started to respond. "Yes, I agree that we get along. And I know there is a physical attraction." Her cheeks turned pink. "But given the fact that I'm likely to be an embarrassment to my husband, I would need to know that, if he can't believe in my gifts, that he'll at least love me enough to accept them on faith."

"Love?" A knot formed in his throat.

"Love. One of those things that, like my gifts, you can't see. Most only believe in it once they have experienced it."

"How do you know if what you feel is love? When you've never experienced it?"

"Experienced what?" a man asked from behind them.

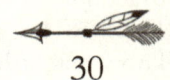

30

"Maska. What are you doing here?" Ahyoka asked.

Maska glanced from one of them to the other. "You're wanted at the gathering place."

"Who?" Kajika asked.

"Both of you." He motioned for the two of them to go ahead of him.

Ahyoka looked at Kajika.

"We'll finish this later," he told her in a lower tone. He took her hand and pulled her with him toward the gathering place.

Maska fell into step on her other side. She searched Maska's face for a hint about why they might be needed but couldn't read anything in his expression.

The three of them marched toward the center of the village in silence. When she saw the size of the crowd that had assembled at the gathering place, she slowed her pace almost to a stop.

"What's going on? Why is everyone here?" she asked.

"My guess is they have nothing else to do," Maska grumbled.

"Are Yonaguska and Winema still sitting near Chief Hiamovi?" Kajika asked as they reached the outer ring of the crowd.

"They should be," Maska answered.

Kajika shouldered his way through the crowd, pulling her behind him until they reached the center. Chief Hiamovi spotted them as soon as they broke through the mass. "There they are!"

Ahyoka glanced up at Kajika. He frowned before he could slip into his formal expression. She'd only seen him use it a few times—mostly when he'd been talking with Chief Hiamovi. She guessed he only did it when he needed to make an effort to not betray what his thoughts really were.

"Come." Chief Hiamovi gestured them forward.

Ahyoka searched the crowd for Winema. She too had a fake smile plastered on her face. Chief Yonaguska looked mildly bored. And her father stood off to one side with his arms folded across his chest. She couldn't read his thoughts at all.

Destiny. The wind spirits' whisper calmed her skittering pulse.

"I understand a celebration is in order for the two of you," Hiamovi said.

"There is?" Ahyoka asked.

"Chief Yonaguska and I have been talking about the possibility of you joining his people as Kajika's wife. I told him that there would be no way that you would turn down such an honor, so yes, I believe we do have a reason to celebrate."

"But I—"

"Ahyoka, dear." Winema hugged her tightly. "Why don't you come and sit with me. I want to hear more about your recent travels." She took her by the hand and pulled her away from the center of the group.

"But—"

"Questions later. Just smile as if you know what's happening," Winema told her in a whisper.

Ahyoka pressed her lips together in what she hoped was something other than a grimace. What was happening? It sounded as if her life had already been decided, even though no one other than Kajika had asked her opinion. How was this to be her destiny?

Questions burned in her gut, but she nodded and followed Winema.

Chief Yonaguska greeted her with a crushing embrace. "Glad to see you weathered your journey well. Kajika told me how you helped find the person responsible for Dyami's death. Our whole village is grateful for everything you did for them."

"You're welcome. I'm glad I could help bring peace to Dyami's family."

"Yes, well, we're glad you weren't hurt in the process." He patted her back. "I've enjoyed meeting your father and brother. It sounds as if we could exchange many hunting stories." Yonaguska gestured at Paco. "Perhaps we could hold a hunt together later this year. Something for the younger ones to join."

"Excellent idea," Hiamovi added.

Paco stepped in and tossed a couple of ideas to Yonaguska. While they were distracted, Kajika snuck up behind Ahyoka and tapped her on the shoulder. He gestured for her to follow him. She looked at Winema for guidance. She winked and shifted so she stood in front of Ahyoka, effectively blocking their escape from view.

She didn't really want to talk to Kajika at that moment, but it would probably be the only way she could get answers. And if anyone deserved to get a taste of her temper, it would be him.

A few people glanced their way as they wove through the crowd, but no one stopped them or called attention to their escape.

When they finally reached an area of the village without anyone nearby, Kajika stopped and faced her. "I'm sorry about all of that." He gestured toward the gathering place. "I didn't mean for this to happen."

She folded her arms. "Mean for what to happen? To give my chief an easy way to get rid of me? Or to announce your plans to everyone in my village before talking with me?"

"Neither," he growled.

He glanced at the people passing by then grabbed her hand and pulled her further away from the crowd.

"I don't know what was said after I came looking for you, but I didn't say anything to Chief Hiamovi about any plans. Of any kind."

"Then why did he make it sound as if there were some kind of agreement?" she asked.

"I don't know. I did talk with Yonaguska about you, but only to get his advice on a few things."

"Things like what?"

"Like whether or not the union would be welcomed by the two villages. The last thing I would want is for you to go from one village where the people treat you like an outcast to another where they treated you no better, or perhaps even worse."

She swayed on her feet. "You think your people would treat me worse?"

"No, actually, I don't. From what I could see of your last visit, they all welcomed you and treated you with respect. But I didn't want any hard feelings to surface if I were to take a wife from another village."

She stepped back. "You mean by other women? Someone who might think you should have picked them instead?"

He dipped his head once, slowly.

"Had you made an agreement with someone else?"

"No. Nothing that serious, but I had been thinking about the idea for some time."

"And people had formed ideas."

He nodded.

"That still doesn't explain why everyone thinks we have agreed to something."

"I won't know until I talk with Yonaguska. But I strongly suspect that your chief made assumptions based on nothing."

She shook her head and looked away. "That is very likely."

He touched her arm. "The reality is I missed you after I returned home."

She looked up at him, afraid to hope.

"You have no idea how many times I wanted to show you something or ask you what you thought. Every day I thought of you. That's why I went to my brother and Yonaguska for advice."

Her heart fluttered in her chest. "What did they tell you?"

"That I should follow my gut. So, I came here to ask if there would be any chance I could get you to consider the idea." He touched her cheek. "I know you said you wanted someone who loved you enough to look past your gifts. I don't think you should have to stoop that low. I may not know much about love, but I know that I want to be with you. Every day. I want to have a future that includes you. Your gifts don't bother me. I may not understand everything you see and hear, but I trust that you wouldn't lie to me about it, and I would be willing to die to protect you from anyone who would wish you harm—because of your gifts or any other reason."

A tear slipped down her cheek.

He wiped it away. "Why do you cry? Did I say something to hurt you?"

"No." She sniffled. "You said everything just right. I just…" She shook her head.

"If I said everything right, then why are you saying no?"

She grabbed his hand. "I'm not." She put her hand on his chest. "I don't need to consider. I love you. I know I do, and I wouldn't mind spending a lifetime teaching you about love. So, yes, I will take you as husband."

He grabbed her and kissed her until neither of them could breathe. When he pulled back, they were both grinning like fools.

Destiny.

"So it is settled then?" He let her slide down his body until her feet touched the ground.

"Well, you will still have to talk with Father."

His tone turned solemn. "I will pay any price he asks of me."

"As long as Ahyoka is happy, I won't ask much of you," Paco said as he approached.

Her cheeks heated. "I'm sorry for sneaking out."

Paco waved her concern away. "I don't blame you. I wish I could sneak away for the rest of the day. But…"

"But they expect us to return," she said, finishing his sentence.

"Yes." Paco looked to Kajika. "There will be time later for the two of you to have time to talk in private."

Kajika nodded then held out his hand for Ahyoka. She smiled and gladly placed her palm against his and returned to the crowd.

31

After the sun went down and the day's festivities slowed to a halt, Ahyoka led Kajika back to their spot near the river. For once, she enjoyed mingling with the people of her village. It may have been because people looked at her as something other than a puzzle. Most likely it had been because Kajika remained by her side throughout the day. She couldn't remember smiling more.

Welcome, Spirit Talker.

Welcome, Warrior.

Ahyoka whispered thanks to the spirits as she placed their sleeping mats on a soft spot of grass. When she'd finished, she headed to the river to join Kajika.

"You said the water helped heal your foot, didn't you?" Kajika asked.

"It's not so much the water as it is the spirits that give the water power."

"Are the spirits always here?" he asked with a grimace.

"There are spirits everywhere. But they know when they are needed and they keep a respectful distance when they're not."

"Good." He reached for her and tugged her closer. She slid her arms up his chest and around his neck.

He lowered his head and nibbled the edge of her lip, making her grin grow even bigger. She sighed as he kissed her slow and deep. The warm glow in her belly spread through her body. When he dragged his lips over to her ear and nuzzled the spot just below it, bumps rippled across her skin.

He pulled back and declared, "I've wanted to do that all day."

"I'm sorry you had to wait."

He jerked his head toward the water. "Let's jump in before I forget why we came down here."

"Was a bath the reason we came?"

"No. But it sounded good." He pulled her dress over her head and let it drop on the ground nearby. "You are beautiful."

Her cheeks warmed. "Thank you." She reached for the closure of his pants then paused. "Do you mind if I do this?"

"You can do anything you like with me."

To reward him, she placed a kiss against his chest. With just a couple of tugs, she loosened the knots on his pants. He helped her push them down over his hips. Her eyes were instantly drawn to his fully erect cock. She'd only seen it a couple of times. Neither time allowed her the chance to truly inspect it.

"What are you thinking?" His voice came out gruff.

She ran her finger down the length. "That I'd like to learn how to pleasure you. Last time you made me feel so many wonderful feelings. I think it's only fair."

His throat bobbed up and down as he swallowed.

Taking his lack of response as approval, she knelt in front of him. She wrapped one hand around him and tested the firmness. How could this part of his body be so soft and flexible one moment, then rigid and firm the next? As she explored the ridges with her fingertip, a drop of fluid appeared at the tip. She ran her thumb over the end then brought her thumb to her mouth. She gauged his reaction before letting her tongue dart out for a taste.

Oddly, he seemed to have stopped breathing, yet his gaze remained riveted on her.

When she licked the end of her thumb, his cock jumped.

She had no warning before he pulled her up off the ground and into his arms. With a determined gait, he marched into the river.

"Did I do something wrong?" she asked.

"No."

About the time she felt the water tickling her backside, he set her on her own feet. The water felt even cooler against her heated flesh.

"The why did you stop me?"

"Because I couldn't take much more of what you were doing."

She looked down. "I'm sorry I—"

"You did nothing wrong." He lifted her chin, forcing her to look at him. "It's been too long since we were together, and I've craved you every day. I promise I will give you a chance to explore and look your fill, but not today. I need you right now."

His lips captured hers. Branding her with heat and passion. Her arms circled his neck and she pressed as close to him as she could. The pull of the water around them swirled as if fueled by the fierceness of their desire.

"Wrap your legs around my waist," he murmured against her lips.

When she did as he'd said, he lowered them both into the water and ran his hands over her back, arms, and legs. Seizing the opportunity, she did the same to him.

"Hold on," he warned as he rose from the water. She pressed kisses against his face as he all but ran to the sleeping mats. Somehow he managed to drop onto the mat without crushing her beneath him.

Then his lips once again found hers. They nipped and teased with their tongues, driving each other wild with need. She grasped at his shoulders, trying to get closer, seeking an anchor in the storm he created within her. Her foot skimmed up and down the back of his leg, seeking more contact with him.

"Is it—" She gasped when he nuzzled her neck and ear. "Is it always this way? This driving madness?"

He lifted his head and looked her in the eye. "I don't know about other couples, but I've only felt this way with you."

Her heart fluttered in her chest. She lifted her lips to his and drove them once again into the flames. His hand slid up the side of her belly to her breast. The rough surface of his palm made her groan as it skimmed across her sensitive nipple. He cupped the base then lowered his head to take the tiny bud into his mouth. He flicked his tongue back and forth over the peak then added pressure as he sucked it in. She arched, silently begging for more.

His hand slid down, over her belly, to the juncture between her legs. Moisture coated her opening, so there was no resistance when his finger slid inside. His lips continued to suckle and flicker across her nipple as he teased that sensitive spot.

She squirmed beneath him, needing more, craving the sensations only he could give her. She clutched the back of his head, afraid he would stop. "Please. I need...," she begged, but didn't really know what to ask for.

"I know what you need," he reassured her. He adjusted his position then slid his cock inside of her. She groaned with pleasure. The weight of his body on hers. The heat between them. The sense of him filling her completely. Everything about it felt right.

When he began to rock back and forth, he stirred up new sensations. Her body tightened and her breath stalled in her chest. She hovered near the edge, caught between need and pleasure while the storm reached its pinnacle. When he arched down and drew her nipple into his mouth, her world exploded into thousands of fragments.

"Kajika," she cried out.

Through the haze of her pleasure, she felt his increased thrusts then the stiffening of his back. He tightened his hold on her and groaned against her neck.

They lay locked in each other's embrace until their world righted and both of them were able to breathe properly. Then he rolled to one side and pulled her snuggly against him.

With the twinkling lights in the night sky above them, they drifted off to dream. To dream of the future they would share and the love that would see them through anything that came their way.

Destiny, Spirit Talker.
Your destiny begins now.

EPILOGUE

"Ahyoka! Ahyoka! Come quickly."

Ahyoka stuck her head out of the flap of her tepee. "Halona? What's wrong? Please tell me your brother didn't get hurt playing stickball again. He wasn't completely healed from his last injury."

The young girl hopped from one foot to the other. "No. It's not him." Excitement rolled off the girl in waves. "Mother said you were needed at the circle. Hurry!"

"All right. I'm coming. Let me get my wrap." Even though winter had mostly passed, the wind still felt chilled. Kajika's mother had sent her one of the most beautiful pieces of weaving she'd ever seen and she treasured it. It also happened to be the only thing long enough to cover her now enormous belly.

With only a short time to go until the baby presented himself, at least according to the wind spirits, she found it hard to wear anything comfortably these days.

She waddled after Halona as fast as she could manage, anxious to see what could have stirred the young girl up so. They passed a few villagers along the way and, thankfully, none of them seemed alarmed by anything. When the circle came into view, Ahyoka could see a small crowd gathered at one edge.

Kajika should have returned from his ride by now. Perhaps he would know what the commotion was about.

As she drew near, the crowd parted to let her in.

"Maska!" she said with surprised delight. "What are you doing here?"

When he stood to greet her, Ahyoka could see he had been tending to a young woman. The woman held a baby and there were two children hovering nearby. Their eyes were wide and they watched everything around them even as they shoveled food into their mouths.

"Wow. You're getting big," Maska said bluntly.

"I am. Thank you for pointing it out." She tipped her head toward the woman. "What's going on?"

"This is Talulah." Maska looked down at the woman then pointed to each of the children in turn. "And these are her brothers, Wynono and Enyeto, and the baby is named Nayati."

"They're not part of Hiamovi's people, are they?" she asked.

His jaw clenched. "No. I came across them a few days ago as I returned from Viho's village." In a lower voice, he told her, "I think someone is chasing them and wants to do them harm."

Danger comes.

Maska flinched.

"I believe you may be right," she murmured. To one of the men gathered nearby, she asked, "Has Kajika returned yet?"

"Yes. I saw him ride in. He's probably still with the horses."

"Would you send one of the boys to find him, please?" She rubbed her belly where the baby kicked her.

After the man turned away, she asked Maska, "You heard them, didn't you?"

"Yes." He grimaced. "More than I want."

She nodded knowingly. "You can learn to block them out."

"I've been doing that for more seasons than I can remember. But it seems I can't any longer."

She patted his arm. "Then try listening to them when they speak and you won't have to fight them."

He frowned at her.

"Maska," Winema called out as she approached. "One of the widows has offered to let them stay with her until we get this sorted out." She shook her head as her gaze landed on the children. "The poor things look nearly worn out."

"The boys have held up pretty well, considering how far they've walked since I found them," Maska said. "But I'm not certain how much farther they had traveled before then."

"We'll make sure they get plenty of food and rest while you and Yonaguska and Kajika work out what should become of them."

Winema patted Maska's arm then bustled off to tend to some detail.

Winema had a gift for making everyone feel welcome. And the guidance she provided to all of the women in the village was invaluable. Knowing Winema would be there when the baby arrived went a long way to easing Ahyoka's fears about becoming a mother.

The prickling of awareness that always alerted her whenever Kajika drew near made her turn and look over her shoulder. She smiled and waited for him to reach her.

Without fail, he slipped his arm about her shoulder and kissed the top of her head. He then extended his free hand to Maska. "This is a pleasant surprise." They gripped each other's forearms.

"Unfortunately it is not a planned visit," Maska confessed.

"Is something wrong?" He cast a worried glance her way.

"We're not certain," she told him. "Maska found a woman and her brothers during his travels. He thinks they're running from someone." She nodded to where the woman and boys were huddled.

Kajika frowned. "What did Yonaguska say?"

"I'm not certain," she told him. "I've only been here long enough to greet Maska." She grimaced. "I'm afraid I don't get from one place to the other as quickly as I used to."

"As long as you don't tire yourself out."

His concern for her and the baby warmed her heart.

"I've only heard Yonaguska give orders to get them some food and water," Maska told him. "Winema has been looking for a place where they can rest."

Kajika nodded. "I'll go talk with him." He dropped another kiss on top of her head then headed toward the group of elders.

"I'll come with you." Maska followed on his heels.

The shaman's time has come.

"He won't like it," she whispered back to the wind.

Destiny waits for no one.

"What of the woman?"

Destiny.

Ahyoka smiled. She couldn't wait to see how Maska's turned out.

THE END

ABOUT THE AUTHOR

Dena Garson is an award-winning author of paranormal, fantasy, steampunk, and sci-fi romance. She holds a BBA and MBA in Business and works in the wacky world of quality and process improvement. Making up her own reality on paper is what keeps her sane.

She is the mother of two rowdy boys and two rambunctious cats (AKA the fuzzy jerks). When she isn't writing you can find her at the sewing machine or stringing beads. She is also a devoted Whovian and Dallas Cowboys fan.

Find Dena on the web at:

Website - https://denagarson.com
Facebook- https://www.facebook.com/AuthorDenaGarson
Email – DenaGarson@gmail.com

Sign up for Dena's newsletter at:
https://landing.mailerlite.com/webforms/landing/v7a2i6

OTHER BOOKS BY DENA GARSON

Paranormal/Fantasy Romance
Ghostly Persuasion
Mystic's Touch
Who Wants Forever
Your Wild Heart (Black Hills Wolves)

Paradise Valley Shifters
Anna's Bear
That Touch of Shifter Silk

Rising Sons Sci-Fi Romance
Rege's Rescue
Vordol's Vow

Royal Intelligence Steampunk Romance
Christmas Royale
Her Clockwork Heart
To London, With Love

Find detailed book information at https://denagarson.com/books